STAR ISLAND

Weekly Reader Children's Book Club presents

STAR ISLAND

❧ ❧

by Louise Dickinson Rich
ILLUSTRATED BY ELINOR JAEGER

FRANKLIN WATTS, INC.
575 Lexington Avenue · New York, N. Y. 10022

SBN 531–01798–2
Library of Congress Catalog Card Number: 68–10661
© Copyright 1968 by Louise Dickinson Rich
Printed in the United States of America
Originally published as *Star Island Boy*
Weekly Reader Children's Book Club Edition
Senior Division

STAR ISLAND

❦❦ CHAPTER 1

Larry Scott sat slouched in the corner of the seat, watching Miss Carr out of the corners of his eyes.

"Just tell me when you see a right turn, Larry. We— Oh, here it is."

She took the turn carefully. She was a very good driver. She had to be. She was a caseworker for the Division of Child Welfare. Her work took her in all kinds of weather over roads good and bad throughout Maine. She had never had an accident. The only thing that made her a little nervous was heavy traffic. Long ago, Larry had learned to keep still when there were stop-and-go signs to be obeyed. In towns and cities, Miss Carr liked to give her whole attention to driving. He knew that she would relax, once they were on the open road. Then she would tell him about the place to which they were going.

"You've never been to the coast, have you, Larry?" Miss Carr asked suddenly.

Larry sat up and glanced out the window. Abruptly

they were passing between late August meadows, and the road ahead was empty of traffic. Now Miss Carr could talk.

"No, ma'am," he answered politely. He had never been anywhere much, except from one inland foster home to another.

"You'll find it strange at first. We're going— Oh, bother!"

They had come over the brow of a hill onto a stretch of road under repair. Miss Carr disliked construction almost as much as she did city traffic. In silence, she picked her way between bulldozers and gravel trucks.

One thing she wouldn't have to tell him, when she could talk again, Larry thought. This would end as these things always ended. Ever since he could remember, he had been moved from one family to another. That was what it meant to be an orphan, a State Kid. You didn't belong anywhere. Nobody wanted you.

When he was small he had believed that somewhere there was a place for him. Every time Miss Carr took him to a new foster home, he had been positive that this would be the one that would last forever. Now that he was eleven, he knew better. When people no longer needed the money that the state paid them for taking care of him, they always found a good excuse to send him away.

This last time the excuse had been that Mrs. White's mother was coming to live with her. A boy around the house would upset the old lady. But Larry had heard Mr. and Mrs. White talking. (Nobody ever told a State Kid anything. To know what was going on, he had to listen when he had a chance. Maybe it was sneaky and wrong, but how else could he find out what was happening?)

Mrs. White's mother was going to pay the Whites well for staying there. They wouldn't need Larry's board money anymore.

Before that, the Frosts had kept him until Mr. Frost got a better job in another city. They had said that it would be bad for Larry to change schools in the middle of the year. He had changed schools plenty of times before. That was just an excuse. The truth was that they no longer needed him.

The Smiths had been a little bit different. They had

3

not needed the money. They had an only child who was just Larry's age. No one would have guessed it. Bobby Smith had been sick for a long time. He was thin and pale, and he tired very quickly. The doctors said that it would be good for him to have a companion, someone to play with him and look out for him until he was strong again. Mrs. Smith had explained it to Larry, and he had been careful to be gentle with Bobby.

Larry had to admit that the Smiths had been good to him. He had thought that they meant to keep him always. What a dope he had been! He should have known that they would let him go as soon as Bobby was well again. Mrs. Smith had cried some when Miss Carr came for Larry, but still she had let him go. She hadn't really cared about him—only about what he could do for Bobby.

All the foster homes before the Smiths' were jumbled up in Larry's mind. It didn't make any difference. They had all been the same. Each time, he had tried to be good, to be obedient and helpful. Each time, he had hoped. Sooner or later, each time, Miss Carr had come for him. He had asked, each time, "Why? What have I done?" He had been too young to understand that there didn't have to be a reason why. Not if you were a State Kid, there didn't have to be.

He wondered what excuse the new people would think up to get rid of him, when the time came. The time would come, of course, no matter how hard he tried to make them like him and want him. Well, this time he just wasn't going to try. He'd be good enough so that they couldn't use his bad behavior as an excuse, and that was all. He was through knocking himself out for something that he never could have.

The road construction was behind them, and Miss Carr drew a deep sigh of relief.

"Well, as I was saying, Larry, you'll find it strange at first. We're going to an island seven miles out to sea."

Larry was horrified. It was bad enough to have to get used to new people and the way that they did things, without being stuck on some stupid island out in the middle of the sea. He'd never been on an island, but he'd heard about them. Sailors got shipwrecked on them and ate raw clams until they were rescued, or died. There was nothing to do on an island except watch the horizon for a sail.

"It's not very large," Miss Carr went on, "only two miles long and about a mile across at the widest part. It's called Star Island, because it's shaped something like a star. The village is Starhaven. It isn't very big, either. There are twenty families there in all."

There had been more than twenty families on the short street where the Whites lived, back in the city. Heck, he'd bet that there were more than that in just one of the big apartment buildings downtown. Miss Carr must be joking.

"Twenty houses don't make a town," he said scornfully.

She laughed. "They do on Star Island. It's a real town, all right. They elect their own town officers, and they have a school and a general store. The post office is in one of the houses, but it's a regular post office all the same. That's all you need to make a town—that and people. There are forty-nine people on Star Island."

"Counting everybody?" Larry asked quickly. "Counting kids?"

"Counting the children," Miss Carr assured him. "There are three children."

"There'll be four, with me," Larry said almost to himself. There'll be three who belong there, he was thinking, and me. Always before, he had managed to lose himself in the group. On the island, he'd stick out like a sore thumb. He'd be the State Kid. He'd be a freak.

Miss Carr smiled. "There'll be eleven."

"But you said—" Larry was puzzled. "You mean there'll be other State Kids?"

"Oh, Larry, Larry," Miss Carr sighed and shook her head, "how often do I have to tell you? *Not* State Kids! Foster children, *please*."

"That's what I meant." He should have remembered how much she disliked the term "State Kid." He did some quick arithmetic in his head. "You mean there'll be eight of us—foster children?"

She nodded. "We're meeting the others at the ferry landing in Stillport. The only way you can get onto

6

an island, you know, if you have been paying attention in geography, is on a boat." She smiled to show that she was teasing him a little.

It's the only way you can get off, too, Larry thought, but he didn't say it out loud.

Miss Carr's voice grew warm. "Oh, Larry, this is going to be wonderful for all of you. I envy you. It's going to be a real adventure, discovering and exploring a whole new world. Just you wait and see."

Larry stared at her in amazement. She really meant what she was saying. She really believed it. She just didn't know what it was like to be a State Kid, in spite of all her years as a social worker.

He'd wait and see, all right. He didn't have any choice. He already knew, though, how this wonderful adventure was going to turn out—with him sitting right in this very car, bound for still another foster home.

❦❦ CHAPTER 2

They arrived in Stillport in the early afternoon.
Larry had a confused impression of driving along a
busy main street, down a short lane, and onto a wharf
of weathered planks. It was perched high above the
water on tall, seaweed-covered stilts. Beyond lay the
harbor, full of anchored boats. Beyond that, an enormous expanse of blue water reached out to meet the
enormous blue sky. Sea gulls filled the air with their
mewing and the white flashing of their wings.

The ferry was a sturdy boat with an open cockpit
and a covered wheelhouse. It was tied up with stout
cables at the end of the landing. Two men in hip
boots, plaid shirts and long-billed caps were transfer-
ring a small mountain of boxes, crates, barrels, and
sacks from the wharf to the boat. Larry hardly saw

8

them. He was much more interested in the group sitting on a bench at the stern of the ferry.

He passed over the woman quickly. She must be the caseworker in charge of the other children. He spared only a glance for the three girls. The one with red hair and freckles was about his own age. The other two were younger, probably around six or seven. But who needed girls? It was the boys who counted.

One of the boys was Larry's age. The other three were much younger. The smallest looked as though he might still believe in a permanent foster home. Poor kid, he'd find out. But before Larry could form any more opinions, Miss Carr was telling him to take his belongings out of the car.

"We'll be sailing as soon as the freight is loaded,"

she said. "Almost everything that the islanders need has to be taken out from the mainland. The ferry makes only two trips a week. That means quite a load on each trip. They raise a few vegetables out on Star, but not nearly enough to supply everybody all year round. Besides, the islanders don't have time to cultivate big gardens."

Larry added his everyday sneakers to his tiny pile of luggage. "I should think they'd have plenty of time. There's nothing to do and no place to go on an island, is there?"

Miss Carr laughed a little helplessly. "Oh, Larry, you don't understand at all. That's my fault. I should have told you more about Star Island. They're lobstermen out there. That's how they earn a living. Every man owns his own boat, and just keeping a lobster boat shipshape is a big job. Then there are so many other chores that everybody on the island is busy all day long. As for places to go—why, the whole ocean is their front yard. It's their world. They can go anywhere they please, so long as there is enough water to float a boat."

Before Larry could answer, one of the men from the ferry came over to them. "We're ready to cast off, Miss Carr," he said, "so if you'll just get aboard." He picked up Larry's old suitcase. "I'll give you a hand, young feller."

He led the way down a steep gangplank and went forward to start the engine. The second man cast off the moorings and leaped nimbly aboard. The motor roared into life, then settled down to a deep, steady purring. The ferry drew away from the landing and threaded its way through the fleet of anchored boats toward the open sea.

"The trip to the island takes over half an hour," Miss Carr said, "so you'll have a chance to start getting acquainted with the other children. This is Larry Scott," she told the other caseworker, "and this is Miss Bridges, Larry. As you know, a worker from the Child Welfare Division visits a foster home regularly. Miss Bridges and I will take turns, out on Star. Now" —she turned to the row of children—"some of you I don't know. The easiest way would be for all of us to introduce ourselves. You are—?" She made the words a question as she nodded to the tall redheaded girl at the end of the bench.

"I'm Sally." The names rippled along the row as Miss Carr nodded to each child in turn. Larry tried to keep them straight. The little boy with the hopeful eyes was Tony. The biggest boy was Tom. The boy with the curly hair was Jack—or was he Ray? The two little girls were Ethel and Jenny, but Larry was not sure which was which.

He would soon be able to put the right name to the right face, he told himself. He'd had enough practice, moving from home to home and school to school. He'd bet he could call hundreds of people by name—maybe even a thousand.

11

Miss Carr and Miss Bridges walked to the bow of the boat and began talking in low tones. Larry sat down beside Tom. "Hi," he said. "How old are you?"

"Twelve," Tom told him. "You?"

"Going on twelve." Larry didn't like to admit that he wasn't quite eleven and a half. "You been a State Kid long?"

Tom looked puzzled. Then he sighed. "State Kid," he said. "I keep forgetting. My folks were killed in an accident this summer, and there wasn't anybody—" His voice trembled, but he went on resolutely. "I stayed with a neighbor of ours for a while, but—"

"Sure, I know." The neighbors had their own families and couldn't be bothered with Tom. "I've been a State Kid all my life."

Tom gave him a look of sympathy. "Miss Bridges makes Star Island sound nice," he ventured. "She says I'll like it after I get used to it. I'm going to try, anyhow. Miss Bridges says I have to adjust."

Larry laughed shortly. "Adjust." That was a favorite word with caseworkers. It meant that you had to try to act like the people you were living with, whether you liked it or not.

"There's something I don't understand, though," Tom was going on. "Why do they want so many of us—" he hesitated a little "—us State Kids? What happened to all the kids that belong out there? You know, the ones that were born there. It seems funny—" His voice trailed off.

That had not occurred to Larry. It did seem funny, come to think about it. Maybe—

Before he could find any explanation, the purring of the engine changed to a deep-throated growl. The boat picked up speed, drawing away from the flock of gulls that had been following it. Turning, Larry saw that they had come out of the harbor and were leaving the mainland behind. All around them was nothing but water, rolling past in green, white-crested waves. The ferry suddenly seemed very small, no bigger and no safer than a nutshell tossing about on the ocean. He wasn't really afraid, he told himself stoutly, but he sure hoped that those men up front knew what they were doing.

Miss Carr was smiling and calling to them. "Children, look! You can see Star Island now. See? Way off there on the horizon."

Larry stood up. To his surprise he found that he couldn't walk straight. When he put his foot down, the deck wasn't there, or else it was there too soon. There must be a trick to getting around on a rolling and pitching boat. The ferrymen walked as easily as though they were crossing a kitchen floor.

He looked where Miss Carr was pointing. At last he made out a dim and faraway shape. It looked more like a small blue cloud on the horizon than like firm, dry land.

"It doesn't look real," Sally's voice said behind him. "It looks like a dream island."

"A fairy island," little Jenny—or Ethel—suggested.

"A magic island," Ethel—or Jenny—chimed in.

Girls! They always had to show off, to talk fancy, like—well, like girls. The island didn't look like any magic island to Larry. It just looked lost and lonely, out there on the edge of the world.

"It's real," Miss Carr assured them. "It isn't a dream."

"But for some of you—for all of you, I hope," Miss Bridges added, "it might be a magic island, especially if you believe that it will be. Magic works best if you believe in it."

Larry snorted softly. Some women talked as silly as girls. He caught Sally's eye, and she surprised him by winking. Maybe she wasn't as silly as she sounded. Maybe she'd learned, as he had, to say what social workers and foster parents expected.

As they drew nearer, the island took on a more solid appearance. The cloudy blue changed slowly to the dark green of trees and the soft pinkish-gray of granite ledges. Soon they could see a lacelike fringe of white spray, where the surf broke against the rocks. Brightly painted bits of wood began to appear on the surface of the sea, first a few and then more and more.

"Those are lobster buoys," Miss Carr explained. "They mark where the lobster traps have been set. You notice that they aren't all painted the same. Each lobsterman has his own colors, so that he can tell which traps are his."

"Where do the people live?" Larry asked. He couldn't see a single house anywhere.

"Starhaven is on the other side of the island. Do you know what 'haven' means? It means 'a place of shelter and safety.' That's just what Starhaven is—a sheltered, snug little harbor. The boats are safe there in any storm."

As if at a signal, a flock of gulls streamed out from the island and circled over the ferry, screaming hoarsely.

"The gulls meet every boat," Miss Bridges said. "They're looking for something to eat. When the lobstermen finish hauling their traps, they throw overboard the leftover fish scraps that they use for bait. That means a fine meal for the gulls."

The gulls suddenly wheeled away and, crying more loudly than ever, set off in pursuit of a small white boat that had appeared around a point.

"That's one of the lobstermen now," Miss Carr said. "Doesn't his boat look tiny? Yet lobster boats can survive rough seas better than many larger vessels. They are built to take punishment. So are the men who own them. They are among the best seamen in the world."

"Hey, look, Larry," Tom exclaimed, "that's a kid running that boat. Heck, I bet he's no older than we are."

Sure enough, the figure at the wheel of the lobster boat was a boy. The man was busying himself at the stern. They were both clad in yellow oilskins, hip boots, and long-billed caps.

"That's Lon Cole and his boy Matt," one of the

ferrymen volunteered. "Matt'll be some old glad to have someone his own age to chum round with. All he's had up to now is Billy Wells—he's only seven— and Linda Allen, who's a girl, as you might surmise." He waved, and the two in the boat waved back.

The lobster boat changed course and came close to the ferry. The boy at the wheel stared up into the faces turned toward him. Looking us over, Larry thought, sizing us up.

Two could play at that game. He scowled down at Matt Cole, and Matt scowled back. Then he did something to the controls. The lobster boat gained speed, swooped once in a tight circle around the ferry, and darted off to the entrance of the harbor.

Showing off, Larry said to himself. The heck with Matt Cole and his boat.

❦❦ CHAPTER 3

The harbor at Starhaven was just what Miss Carr
had said it would be—a safe and quiet shelter. The
slow pounding of the sea beyond the narrow entrance
sounded loud, but here it was calm. The reflections
of the lobster boats lying at their moorings were clear
and unwavering in the still water. All around the
harbor's shore were long-legged wharves like those
Larry had seen in Stillport. On some of them were
piles of what looked like wooden cages with rounded
tops. They, Larry guessed, were lobster traps.

Behind the wharves were some unpainted shacks
that seemed to be workshops. Their walls were hung
with gay lobster buoys. A row of gulls, all facing the
same way into the wind, perched on the ridgepole
of each shack. The houses of the village were scattered
on the steeply rising ground above the harbor. Most
of them were painted white, with small windows peer-
ing out from under high, pointed roofs. They were

plain little buildings, but they looked neat and trim.

Larry wondered which one was going to be his new foster home. Then he laughed silently at himself. What difference did it make? He wasn't going to be here long enough for it to matter.

The ferry drew alongside the largest wharf, which Miss Carr said was the town landing. A small crowd was gathered on it now.

"Everybody in town is here," Miss Bridges said. "I'm not surprised. They've all been looking forward to your arrival. It's a big day for Star Island."

Why? Larry wondered, faintly troubled. Why were the islanders so eager to provide homes for so many homeless children?

The ferrymen tossed the mooring lines up onto the landing. One of them was caught by a boy, who dropped it in expert loops over a stout post. It was Matt Cole again, Larry observed. He was making a big deal out of a simple thing like tying up one end of a boat. Larry could feel in his bones that he and Matt were not going to get along well together.

The children were collecting their belongings. Larry picked up his suitcase and few parcels. Then he glanced up at the people standing on the wharf.

They all looked alike to him. All the men were dressed the same, in rubber boots, flannel shirts, and caps. They were all lean and muscular, and all their faces were hard and deeply tanned. Their eyes gazed straight out from beneath the visors of their caps as

19

though they were used to long distances. They all looked tough and capable.

The women were less alike. Some of them were slender and some were plump. Most of them wore cotton dresses, but a few were in dungarees. Some had long hair, drawn back neatly into buns, and some had short hair, blowing about their faces. The faces themselves were different. Some were gentle and smiling, and some were keen and serious. But for all their differences, the women had something in common, like sisters of the same family. Like the men, they all looked capable.

"I'll introduce you to the Chandlers, with whom you're going to live," Miss Carr told Larry. "Then I'll have to help Miss Bridges with her charges. I'll see you later. You'll be all right. The Chandlers are fine people. You'll like them."

Maybe he would and maybe he wouldn't, Larry thought. Either way, there wasn't anything he could do about it. He followed Miss Carr up the gangplank and along the wharf to where a man and a woman were standing together.

"So this is Larry!" the woman said immediately. She had a pleasant, almost square face and a comfortable manner. There was something about her dark eyes and firm jaw, though, that suggested that she would take no nonsense from anybody. "We're glad you're here, Larry. We hope you'll be happy with us."

"That goes for me, too." Mr. Chandler held out his

hand, smiling. His eyes were a startling blue in his dark face. His handclasp was warm and strong. "You go along with Ma up home, and I'll be along as soon as we get the boat unloaded." He pronounced "boat" so that it sounded more like "but," and "unloaded" like "unludded." "The boys have to get back to the main- land, so we all turn to and help." He squeezed Larry's shoulder and strode off down the landing.

"Let's go," Mrs. Chandler said briskly. "The sooner we get your gear stowed, the sooner you'll feel at home. Here, give me a couple of those bundles. We live at the top of the road"—she made it sound like "rud"—"and it's a fair-to-middling haul."

They sure talked funny out here on Star Island. Larry supposed that "getting his gear stowed" meant "putting his things away," and that "a fair-to-middling haul" was "a medium—long distance." Maybe he'd get used to the talk if he stayed long enough.

Some of the other children, he saw, were already leaving the landing with island women. Sally was talk- ing to a strange girl who must be the Linda mentioned by the ferryman. Tom was laughing at something that a tall woman was saying. Everybody seemed to fit right in—everybody except him.

He fell into step with Mrs. Chandler. "I'll show you the points of interest," she said, laughing, as they left the wharf. "Such as they are. When you come right down to it, Starhaven is pretty much of a muchness. But we like it—wouldn't live anywhere else for love nor money. That's the store." She pointed to a large, low building with big windows on either side of the door. "This is the main street. To tell the truth, it's the only street."

It wasn't a street at all, in Larry's opinion. It was just a wide dirt road wandering up the hill between outcroppings of rock and flaming flower beds. They were like brilliant patchwork quilts of scarlet and blue, purple and gold flung down on the ledges in front of the houses. Everybody had flower gardens. It was a good thing that they did, Larry thought. They didn't seem to have much else on Star Island.

There were no sidewalks. People were walking smack in the middle of the road, as though they'd never heard of getting run over. Of course, there were no cars in sight right now. There hadn't been any down at the landing. There were none parked in the driveways of the houses they were passing, either. Then he noticed that there weren't even any driveways or any garages.

His curiosity got the better of him. "Where do people park their cars here?" he asked.

Mrs. Chandler acted surprised. "Oh, there aren't any cars on Star. A few of us keep them in Stillport, in case we want to travel around on the main. That's what we call the mainland—the main. But we don't have any use for them here. It's only a mile to the farthest part of the island in any direction. Just a comfortable stroll. There aren't any roads anyhow—just this street."

That partly explained the odd, empty look of the street. But something else was missing. Telephone poles! Didn't they even have telephones here?

"No," Mrs. Chandler said when Larry asked. "It's only a step from house to house, so we don't need phones. We all have walkie-talkies and shortwave radios. That way, we can talk to our men when they're out hauling their traps, or to the Coast Guard in an emergency. In the old days, Star was pretty much cut off from the world, but not now."

Perhaps she didn't think so, Larry told himself, but the island seemed pretty cut off—as she called it—to him. Ahead, he saw Tom and the tall woman turn in at a white house. They were chattering away like old friends. The sight made Larry feel more alone than ever. Well, Tom would learn not to talk so freely to foster parents. It didn't pay. They used what you said against you, when they got a chance.

"Here's the school," Mrs. Chandler interrupted his thoughts. The school was a small, gray-shingled building with a flagpole in front. "It doesn't open until next week, so you'll have time to get acquainted with the island before then. The teacher won't be over till the Friday ferry."

They walked on in silence for a moment. Larry noticed that several of the houses were unoccupied, their windows staring out emptily over harbor and sea.

"You've seen the whole of Starhaven," Mrs. Chandler said. Then her face lighted and shone. "Except home," she added. "That's home, dead ahead."

❧❧ CHAPTER 4

The house was like the others, trim and white. A low ell extended from one side. Like the others, the house was surrounded by flowers. A tortoiseshell cat slept in the sun on the stone doorstep, and a big black dog came bounding around the corner as they approached.

"I suppose I ought to take you in the front door, the first time," Mrs. Chandler remarked cheerfully, "but we're not very fierce for front doors on Star, except for company. You're not company. You're family, so we'll start the way we're going on and use the kitchen door."

She led the way to the door of the ell, stooping to stroke the cat. "This is Boots," she told Larry. "The smartest cat in Maine, if I do say so." She snapped her fingers, and the dog came to attention on the path below them. "And this is Mate. Mate, shake hands with Larry."

The big dog obediently lifted a paw. Larry, feeling a little foolish, shook it. He had never lived with anybody who owned a dog. Mate searched Larry's face with enormous brown eyes. Then he whined softly and laid his head against Larry's knee.

"Look at that!" Mrs. Chandler exclaimed. "He's taken to you right off. You're going to be great friends, I can see that."

She opened the door. "Nobody locks their doors around here. For one thing, we don't have anything worth stealing, and for another, nobody'd steal it anyhow. Half of us are first cousins, and you don't steal from relatives. Well, come in, come in."

Larry started to follow her. Then he turned back. Mate was looking at him with a question in his eyes. What did you do when a dog looked at you like that? Larry didn't know. His hand went out almost by itself and rested on Mate's huge head. The plume of a tail began to wag, slowly at first and then with frantic joy. Suddenly Larry felt good. Maybe Mrs. Chandler was right. Maybe he and Mate were going to be friends.

Mrs. Chandler had called the room that they entered "the kitchen." It didn't look like any kitchen Larry had ever seen. Windows filled three sides of it. The blank end was occupied by a big black iron cookstove with a huge woodbox beside it. There was an iron sink with a hand pump under the windows overlooking the village and harbor. Wherever Larry had lived before, cooking had been done by gas or

26

electricity, and water had come out of faucets. Still, he recognized the stove and the sink as belonging in a kitchen.

An oval table covered with a red-and-white-checked tablecloth occupied the middle of the room. On it were salt and pepper shakers, a sugar bowl, and a heavy glass jar full of knives, forks, and spoons. The Chandlers must use this as a dining room, too.

And as a living room. In a corner between two windows was a comfortable armchair. A table heaped with magazines and books stood beside it. A rocking chair with a basket of mending on the floor next to it faced another window. A rather battered desk, stacked with papers, filled one wall space. One windowsill held a transistor radio. The TV set must be in another room, Larry decided.

Mrs. Chandler seemed to read Larry's thoughts. "Out here, folks just about live in their kitchens," she said, "except for sleeping. We've all got dining rooms and parlors, but we don't use them much, except for weddings and funerals. A kitchen seems more natural-like, somehow."

Larry wondered if Miss Carr knew about this. When you'd been a State Kid all your life, you learned a few things. One thing Larry had learned was that caseworkers were fussy about the homes in which they placed children. Even the Whites, who had been quite poor, hadn't lived in the kitchen. Maybe when

Miss Carr found out, she'd take him away from this awful island.

Outside, Mate barked once.

"Land!" Mrs. Chandler exclaimed. "Here's Pa now. I meant to show you your room—" She bustled around, putting a stick of wood in the stove and opening the drafts so that the fire roared. "Usually he stays around the store gabbing with the other men until dear knows when. But I guess there wasn't much gabbing today. Too much excitement at home, with all you children coming."

Mr. Chandler came in, moving quietly for all his size. "Well, young feller," he said, "it's good to have you aboard. You probably feel like a cat in a strange garret now, but you'll shake down in no time. If anything puzzles you, don't be afraid to ask questions. We'll do the same. The sooner we understand each other, the better. First question I want to ask you, do you like lobster stew? Because I surmise that's what we're having for supper."

Larry couldn't help laughing. It wasn't the sort of question foster parents usually asked. Usually they wanted to know things like where you had lived last, or how old you were, or even what happened to your parents. Things that they knew the answers to already, or that were none of their business.

"I don't know, Mr. Chandler," he said. "I never ate lobster."

"Never ate lobster?" Mr. Chandler seemed shocked.

28

"Then we'd better start making up for lost time. You've sure got a treat in store for you." He sat down in the armchair and pulled off his boots. "Another thing. This 'Mr. Chandler.' Makes me want to look behind me to see who you're talking to. I don't suppose you want to call us Ma and Pa first off. How's Uncle Joe and Aunt Emma for a starter?"

Foster parents often wanted to be called "uncle" and "aunt." Larry guessed he had more fake aunts and uncles than anybody in the world. Habit made it easy for him to say, "All right, Uncle Joe. That'll be fine."

"Now we've got that settled, how about handing me my slippers there by the woodbox, Larry? Thank you. I'll talk to you about that woodbox tomorrow. It's going to be your job to keep it filled. I've been doing it since our youngest went over to the main, and

I'll be some old happy to be shut of that chore."

Now, Larry thought, I'll see whether he meant what he said about questions. Youngest, he'd said. That meant there were more than one. "How many children do you and Aunt Emma have?" Larry asked carefully.

"Two—a boy and a girl. Good young ones, too, if I do say it."

"What happened— Where—?" Larry didn't quite know how to ask.

"What happened to them?" Uncle Joe was cheerful about it. "That's something maybe you can explain to me, after you've been here for a while. Same thing that happened to all the young people on Star and on lots of other islands, too. They went over to the main to high school. After they saw how folks live there, there was no holding them. They got used to television and movies and steam-heated houses and hot running water and all, and the way we live here seemed pretty slow to them. Slow and hard. So they all cleared out as soon as they could. There are only three left on Star, and I surmise they'll leave as soon as they're old enough."

"Now, Pa," Aunt Emma objected, "that ain't quite fair. You're making it sound like the only thing the young ones were interested in was skylarking around having a high old time. Our own have worked hard and done well for themselves. You're as proud of them as I am. You think they're the white hen's chickens."

"Yup," Uncle Joe agreed roundly. "Martha's married to a mainlander and lives out west," he explained to

Larry, "and Carl is in Texas working for the government. I'm proud of them, I don't deny it. Only it seems a shame—"

"You see, Larry," Aunt Emma interrupted, "we've got a good life here on Star Island. We'd like to know that it will keep on the same after we're gone. It won't —not with the young folks all going over to the main as soon's they've shed their milk teeth. They claim that the world moves on and they want to move with it. Maybe they're right. But I can see the day"—she gazed out the window at the village below—"the day when every house down there, instead of just four or five, will be empty, and there'll be nothing living on Star except gulls and fish crows."

There was a knock at the door, and Miss Carr's voice asked, "May I come in? Lon Cole is waiting to take me and Miss Bridges back to Stillport, but I wanted to check—"

"Everything's fine," Aunt Emma assured her. "Come in and set a minute."

Miss Carr seated herself in the rocking chair and glanced around the room. She used what Larry privately called "the caseworker look." It observed everything, even things behind closed doors, he almost believed. To his surprise, she seemed completely satisfied with what she saw.

"Well, Larry," she said, "we've known each other for a long time, so I don't have to make my little speech to you."

Larry grinned. He couldn't help it. He knew that

speech by heart. It was full of words like "adjust" and "cooperate," "helpful" and "obedient."

"I'll tell you this instead, although probably I shouldn't," Miss Carr went on. "I haven't always been entirely happy about some of the foster homes in which I've left you. This time I am happy. I really envy you, as I said before. You're going to have a wonderful life here in Starhaven."

Sure, Larry thought. So wonderful that the kids who were born and brought up here couldn't stand it. Who did Miss Carr think she was kidding?

Larry relaxed a little over supper. The lobster stew was delicious, faintly pink and dotted with freckles of butter. The Chandlers didn't act as though he were either company or a curiosity. They talked easily about events of the day, interrupting each other occasionally to explain something to him. Best of all, Mate of his own accord lay down as close as he could get to Larry's chair. All through the meal, his eyes remained fixed on Larry's face. When Larry, pretending to scratch his own leg, scratched instead the big dog's ears, Mate's tail wagged enthusiastically. There was no doubt about it, Mate really did like him.

Dessert was deep-dish apple pie, warm from the oven. Larry scraped his plate and said, "I guess that was the best supper I ever ate, Aunt Emma." He meant it, too. Aunt Emma smiled, but before she could answer, the door burst open noisily.

It was Matt Cole, acting—Larry thought resentfully

—as if he owned the place. He glanced at Larry and said breezily, "Hi, Aunt Em. Got a piece of that pie for me? Ah, Mate, old-boy-old-boy-o! What's the good word?"

Mate scrambled up from beside Larry. He was wagging all over and pretending to growl. Matt rough-housed the dog briefly and said, "That's enough. Lie down and behave."

Mate flopped down, rolled over on his back, and waved his front paws in an idiotic manner. He looked so silly and so pleased with himself that everybody except Larry laughed.

Larry didn't join in. He knew that he was being a sorehead, but he couldn't help it. Everything had been going so well, and then Matt had to come in and spoil it. In one minute flat he had made Mate forget all about Larry and had caused Aunt Emma to bustle around getting milk and pie for Matt as though he were the king of England. Who did he think he was anyhow, calling her Aunt Em? Why didn't he go home where he belonged and eat his own mother's pie?

Matt finished his milk, set the glass down with a thump, and for the first time addressed Larry directly. "Aunt Em said—"

There it was again. Aunt Em! Matt must have heard Larry call Mrs. Chandler Aunt Emma and was making fun of him. Larry had met that sort before—kids who delighted in picking on a new boy.

Matt went on smoothly, "—she was giving you Carl's room. It's neat, huh?"

"Larry hasn't seen it yet," Aunt Emma explained. "I meant to— But with one thing and another—"

"Hey, come on, then!" Matt jumped up. "These your things? I'll help you carry them up and unpack them."

Oh, no, you don't, Larry thought. You're not going to paw my stuff over and tell everyone I've got only two sets of underwear.

Aloud he said, "No, thanks. I'll do it myself later."

His tone must have been even more surly than he had intended, because everyone looked at him in surprise. Aunt Emma started to say something, but changed her mind when Uncle Joe cleared his throat loudly. Matt looked as though he had been slapped. It would do him good, Larry thought with satisfaction. It was time someone took him down a peg.

After a little silence, Matt said, "Well, I guess I'll be going home. Come on, Mate. Walk me down the hill." He went out with the dog at his heels.

Three hours later, lying in bed, Larry couldn't go to sleep. The windows under the eaves were still pale rectangles. There had been no television to watch. There wasn't a set on the whole island. Aunt Emma had said that on Star they went to bed before it was dark under the table. Uncle Joe had added that they pried the sun up in the morning. Larry supposed that meant that they all got up before sunrise. He wasn't used to such early hours.

That wasn't what was keeping him awake, though.

34

It wasn't the strange surroundings, either. Larry couldn't remember a more comfortable bed. It was soft and wide, and covered with a bright patchwork quilt. The room was all right, too. The ceiling sloped on the sides, so that it was almost like a cozy cave looking out over the village and the sea. Anywhere else, Larry decided, he would have liked the room.

If only it weren't so quiet! That was what was keeping him awake—the almost frightening stillness. There were no sounds of cars stopping or starting, no footsteps going along a pavement, no voices next door, talking and laughing. Strain his ears as he might, all he could hear was the faint sighing of the wind and the deep, steady rumbling of the surf on the outer reefs.

His thoughts turned to the other people sleeping under this roof. Aunt Emma and Uncle Joe hadn't said anything about his rudeness to Matt, but he could tell that they hadn't liked it. Matt had managed to put him in the wrong all the way round. He had won the Chandlers' sympathy and topped that off by walking away with Mate. One of these days, Larry promised himself, he'd get even with Matt Cole. He'd show him! Somewhat comforted by this unfriendly thought, he closed his eyes resolutely.

But still sleep would not come. Larry got out of bed quietly and went to the window. There wasn't a light in the village—not a streetlight or a single glowing window. All he could see was the dark loom of the land against a dull-silver ocean. The sky was full of stars—brighter, closer stars than Larry had ever known. By their dim light he could make out a smudged band on the horizon. That was the mainland, so terribly far away. As he crept back to bed, he wished with all his heart that he were there.

He was almost asleep when something cold touched his cheek. He stiffened, holding his breath. A ghost? A bear that had somehow sneaked into the house? Or something too horrible to imagine?

Then he heard a soft whine and the thump of a strong tail beating the floor. The bed shook as Mate jumped onto it, turned around and around, then curled up beside him.

Larry let out his breath. "Oh, Mate!" he whispered, and threw his arms around the big dog. "Oh, Mate— Mate—"

Then suddenly they were both fast asleep.

❧❧ CHAPTER 5

Larry was wakened by Mate's rough tongue licking his face. It must be very early, he thought drowsily. The room was barely light. Still, he could hear the rattle of pots and pans from downstairs, and Mate plainly thought it was time to get up. Larry rolled out of bed and dressed quickly.

In the kitchen he found Aunt Emma at the stove, turning blueberry pancakes. Uncle Joe was seated at the table, eating them. If they had been upset by Larry's conduct last night they had forgotten it this morning. They both started talking at once.

Aunt Emma said, "If you want hot water to wash with, there's plenty in the teakettle." Larry had found out the night before that the kitchen served as a washroom in addition to everything else.

"Before you pull up to the table," Uncle Joe requested, "let Boots in, will you, Larry?" Then he saw Mate. "I thought you were out chasing rabbits. Slept on your bed, I suppose?" he asked Larry.

Larry, splashing icy pump water on his face, nodded.

He hoped he wasn't getting Mate into trouble. Maybe there was a rule against his sleeping on beds.

There didn't seem to be.

"He always slept there when Carl was home. He hasn't been upstairs once since Carl left." Aunt Emma rubbed the dog's shaggy head roughly. "Seems good to have a boy in the house again, don't it, old feller?"

"The time to start making a lobsterman out of you is right this very morning," Uncle Joe said. "I thought I'd take you out hauling with me."

"There's no law that says you have to go," Aunt Emma assured Larry. "Maybe you'd rather explore the island today."

Larry tasted a pancake, dripping with butter and maple syrup. It was as good as the lobster stew had been last night.

"I'd like to go," he heard himself saying.

Then he remembered, a little too late, that yesterday he had decided not to adjust and cooperate anymore. Maybe getting up so early had dimmed his wits. Well, being agreeable just once probably wouldn't hurt.

When Larry and Uncle Joe arrived at the harbor, the rosy dawn was full of the sound of powerful motors warming up. Larry was wearing Carl's outgrown hip boots and oilskins. Mate was close at his heels.

"Does everybody here go to work before sunrise?" Larry asked.

"The wind comes up with the sun," Uncle Joe explained. "By noon, it's apt to be pretty choppy outside. We aim to be back home before then." He led the way to a small rowboat drawn up on the shore. "Get in and sit down, Larry. Not you, Mate. You're staying ashore today."

Uncle Joe shoved the skiff into the water, took up the oars, and began rowing with short, strong strokes. Mate barked frantically, then seemed to shrug his shoulders as he started back up the road. He had disappeared by the time Larry and Uncle Joe reached the *Petrel,* Uncle Joe's lobster boat.

"Climb aboard," Uncle Joe directed. He tied the skiff to a floating buoy and clambered into the *Petrel.* "Now stand by and I'll show you how to start this tub."

Larry could tell by Uncle Joe's tone that he was proud of his boat, even if he did call her a tub. He watched carefully as Uncle Joe adjusted knobs and levers, and finally stepped on the starter. The motor purred into instant life.

"Cast off the line," Uncle Joe ordered, and then smiled at Larry's puzzled expression. "I mean, untie that rope up front. You'll learn sea lingo in no time. You're going to be a big help to me."

Once they were on their way out of the harbor, Larry had time to examine the boat. A glass shield and a small roof protected the steersman from wind and spray, but the rest of the boat was open to sky and sea. Wooden tubs stood about the deck. Some were empty, and some contained an evil-smelling hash of decayed fish that must be the lobster bait Miss

Bridges had spoken of yesterday. The engine was under a wooden box in the center of the craft. Beside it was a spool-like drum. There was a pulley built on an arm projecting from the side of the wheelhouse. At the stern, a short mast supported a furled sail. It all looked simple and businesslike, but Larry hadn't the least idea how anything worked. He'd find out, he supposed.

The deck underfoot began to rise and fall, and Larry saw that they had left the harbor behind. A boy waved from a nearby boat. It was Tom, looking unfamiliar in oilskins. He seemed happier than he had yesterday. Larry waved back. Then the two boats veered apart.

"I've got a gang of traps over by Roaring Bull Ledge," Uncle Joe shouted over the noise of the motor. "We'll start there. My buoys are red and white. See how quick you can spot one."

Larry strained his eyes. The whole sea was as many-colored as a rainbow, reflecting the sunrise. There were no buoys that he could see, though. Then the sun burst over the horizon, and the sea turned green. Sharp and clear against the glittering water was a speck of red and white. Larry shouted and pointed.

"Good boy!" Uncle Joe exclaimed. "You saw her soon as I did, and I knew where to look. You've got regular seaman's eyes."

He was not being polite. He meant what he said. Larry had a sudden conviction that Uncle Joe always meant what he said. It was a good thing to know.

40

The *Petrel* slowed and drew alongside the buoy. Uncle Joe picked up a boathook—a long pole with a hook on the end—and caught the line attached to the buoy. Quickly he hitched the line to the pulley and spool, and moved a lever. The spool turned, and the line tightened and began reeling in.

"Man and boy, I've been lobstering for fifty years, Larry," Uncle Joe remarked thoughtfully, "and I still get excited every time I haul a trap—wondering what's in it. Might be almost anything—a new kind of sea creature that nobody's ever heard of, for instance, or a diamond necklace someone dropped overboard from an ocean liner. Or it might be nothing at all. I guess the suspense is what keeps us lobstermen going. That and being our own bosses. Don't know what else it could be. Oh, the money's good. But lobstering is a hard, dangerous life. Most of us could earn more ashore, and easier and safer, taking orders from someone else— Whoops, here she comes!"

The cagelike trap swam up out of the green depths into the light. Uncle Joe swung it aboard with a splashing of seawater. Without Carl's slicker and boots, Larry would have been soaked to the skin.

Examining the trap at close quarters, Larry saw that the ends held funnel-shaped nets. Between them, in the center of the trap, was a bag of coarse mesh. Uncle Joe explained that this was a bait bag, and that the funnels were called trap heads.

"Lobsters aren't very smart, Larry. They scent the

41

bait and crawl in the big ends of the funnels to get it. No reason why they can't crawl out the same way, except that they ain't got the sense to figure that out."

He reached into the trap and took out a large green lobster. The shells from the stew last night had been red. Lobsters were naturally green, Uncle Joe explained. Cooking them turned them red.

"If they're too small, the law says we have to throw them back," he went on, taking a metal measure out of his pocket. "You measure from the eye to the end of the body. This one's a keeper."

He wedged one of the claws with a small wooden plug. "That's the business claw. We plug 'em so they won't take a nip out of us." Then he tossed the lobster into one of the empty tubs and reached into the trap again. This time he pulled out a big starfish, which he tossed overboard in disgust. Larry had thought it rather pretty, but he didn't say so. It might sound silly.

"If you want to make yourself useful," Uncle Joe said, "you can fill bait bags." He handed Larry the bag that he had removed from the trap. Larry looked at it helplessly. "Here, I'll show you." Uncle Joe scooped up a handful of bait and stuffed it into the bag. "Go ahead. It don't smell like the perfumes of Araby, but it won't hurt you."

Larry dipped his hand into the bait tub carefully. The odor was terrible. For a moment he thought he was going to be sick. Then he filled his lungs with clean, salt air and felt better. Uncle Joe was looking at him with approval, but all he said was, "You'll do." He put the bag back into the trap, tossed the trap overboard, and started the *Petrel* again.

All morning long, they cruised from buoy to buoy. The sun rose higher into the sky. The sea turned from green to blue and purple. Whitecaps began to appear on the crests of the waves. Once they were near enough to the mainland so that Larry could make out the houses of Stillport, like toy houses in a toy town. Once they were almost out of sight of land, except for the back of Star Island. It looked wild and deserted. They could have thought themselves the only persons left in the world, if it hadn't been for the sight of other, distant lobster boats going about their business.

At some time during the morning, Larry discovered that he didn't mind the smell of the bait anymore. He didn't even notice it. At about the same time, he found himself getting excited, as Uncle Joe did, each time they pulled a trap aboard. This was fun! There were all sorts of odd things in the traps—fish, prickly little sea urchins, big crabs, and peculiar creatures called sea cucumbers. And of course, lobsters.

"One thing I'll say," Uncle Joe told him. "You're no Jonah. This is about the best haul I've had all summer." Larry felt pleased and proud. "We'll pick up the string at Old Maid's Reef, and then we're done." Uncle Joe sounded well satisfied.

The sun was straight overhead now, and the sea was rough. Star Island looked like a paper cutout pasted

43

against the sky. Uncle Joe turned the bow of the *Petrel* toward it.

"She's breezing up a mite," he said. "I'll hoist the riding sail. A boat handles better in a breeze with a sail. Here, you take the wheel."

Larry looked at him in astonishment.

"Nothing to it, really," Uncle Joe informed him. "See that highest point of the island? Just you keep the bow headed straight at it. You don't have to pull and haul on the wheel. Easy does it." He walked back to the stern.

Larry knew an instant's panic. What if the engine stopped, or a ledge suddenly appeared before him? What would he do?

Then his nervousness left him. The motor was beating like a strong and steady heart, and Uncle Joe would have told him about any ledges. He moved the wheel slightly. The bow of the *Petrel* swung obediently. This wasn't so hard. All he had to do was keep her headed straight for that highest peak.

Larry's eyes were watering when Uncle Joe came forward to stand beside him. He'd hardly dared to blink for fear of wandering off course.

"You're doing fine," Uncle Joe said. "Keep her steady as she goes. I'll take over when we go into the harbor. The channel's a mite tricky till you know it. Right now I'll start cleaning up this mess."

He dipped a pail of water from over the side and began to swab down the deck with an old broom.

As they drew closer to the island, other boats joined them. Everyone was on the way home. Larry saw Tom. He was throwing old bait overboard to the congregation of gulls that had appeared out of nowhere. Larry didn't dare take a hand from the wheel to attract his attention. He contented himself with hoping hard that Tom would notice him.

Yesterday—only yesterday—both he and Tom had been pretty much impressed to see Matt Cole handling a boat.

Well, today he, Larry Scott, was handling a boat himself.

❧❧ CHAPTER 6

The twice-weekly arrival of the ferry with the mail, supplies, and gossip from the mainland was always a big event in Starhaven. This Friday it was even bigger than usual. Everybody was curious to see what Miss Mills, the new teacher, was like.

She proved to be a pretty young woman with a brisk air about her. Being inspected by the entire population of the island didn't seem to bother her a bit. She smiled at Larry, Tom, and Sally, who were standing near the gangplank, spoke to the ferrymen about her baggage, and went off up the road with the Vances. Horace Vance was chairman of the school committee. Miss Mills was to live with his family.

"Well, what do you think?" Tom asked the other two.

"She means business," Sally said promptly. "Did you see her chin? She won't stand any horsing around."

Larry agreed. He had to admit that Sally was smart,

even if she was a girl. "How do you like it here?" he asked her now.

"Best home I ever was in," she told him, "and I've been in a lot. They really seem glad to have us here."

That reminded Larry of something. "I've found out what became of their own kids," he informed Tom. "Nothing, really. They just grew up and went away."

"Yeah, I know," Tom said.

"That's the story anyhow." Sally looked thoughtful. "It still doesn't explain why they wanted so many of us at once."

"They need the money," Larry said positively. "What else could it be?"

"They don't need the money." Sally was very sure of herself. "I'm dumb about a lot of things, but I'm bright about money and people. Everyone says so. So take my word for it, it isn't money."

"Then what else could it be?" Larry asked.

"I've got a theory about that," Sally told them.

"Maybe they miss their own children," Tom suggested. "Maybe they're lonesome for kids."

Larry said nothing. When Tom had been shifted around a few times, he'd get over his soft ideas. He'd find out for himself that nobody cared about State Kids.

"Hi," a new voice said. It was Matt Cole. "You fellers want to go clamming? The tide is right and I know a place—"

"No," Larry said rudely just as Tom said, "Yes."

Matt looked at Larry as if about to speak. Then he shrugged. He and Tom walked away together.

"You didn't have to be so nasty about it," Sally snapped. "What have you got against Matt, anyhow?"

"He thinks he's King of the Mountain around here."

"No, he doesn't. He's all right. He's trying to be friendly. Why don't you take the chip off your shoulder?"

"Why don't you mind your own business?"

Sally scowled at him. "All right for you," she said, and turned on her heel. "Hey, Matt, can I come, too?" She started running after the two boys.

Larry followed more slowly. The three ahead of him had their heads together, talking and laughing. They didn't look back. Suddenly he felt very lonely. Maybe he should have gone with them. He dismissed the idea angrily. He didn't have to jump every time Matt Cole spoke. He didn't need Matt, or the others, either. He had Uncle Joe and Aunt Emma and Mate. Aunt Emma had said it was good to have a boy in the house again, and she'd meant it. She and Uncle Joe and Mate liked him.

He stopped short in the middle of the road. They really did like him. He could tell. Maybe Tom had been right. Maybe the islanders wanted nothing except to share their homes with homeless children.

He started walking again, turning over this new idea in his mind. The more he thought about it, the more he was inclined to believe that Tom just could be right. His steps quickened. He'd go home and see if there wasn't something he could do for Aunt Emma.

But when he arrived at the house on the top of the hill, Aunt Emma wasn't there. Her old straw hat and the blueberry pail were gone from the hook by the door, and Mate was nowhere around. Even Boots was away on some errand of her own. The house was empty and silent except for the singing of the teakettle on the stove and the distant sound of the surf, drifting in through the open windows.

For a moment Larry's heart sank. He had been so sure Aunt Emma would be there with some chore for him to do. He wanted to show her and Uncle Joe that he appreciated them.

Then his spirits rose. He'd surprise them. He'd fill the woodbox clear to the ceiling and tidy up the woodshed. Uncle Joe had said only yesterday that it needed it. Maybe he'd even have time to do some weeding in the flower beds, Larry thought. He had watched Aunt Emma working there the evening before, so he knew what plants not to pull up. She had said then, only half joking, that she was getting to the age when stooping bothered her.

His surprise was successful beyond his fondest hopes. Aunt Emma, carrying her pail full of berries, stopped short when she saw the neat flower beds.

"Now that's what I call a good job," she declared. "I do thank you, Larry. You couldn't have done anything that would have pleased me more."

Larry couldn't remember ever in his life feeling so proud.

School started on Monday. It was different from any school Larry had ever attended. He was used to large buildings where each grade was in a room by itself. Those schools had modern equipment—drinking fountains in the halls, movie projectors, science laboratories, gymnasiums, and even television sets for educational programs.

The Starhaven school had only one room. The only equipment—if you didn't count books, pencils, and paper—was a blackboard, a large globe, and a bucket of water on the shelf by the door. The eleven pupils were seated according to age, the younger ones at the front, the older ones behind them.

There didn't even seem to be any grades. Miss Mills asked some questions, gave some tests, and then put each in the group where she thought he belonged. At the end of the first day Larry, who was a slow reader, found himself in the reading class with little Tony and Ethel. Being best in arithmetic didn't quite make up for that.

He complained about the grading at supper that night. "She's got me stuck in with the babies in reading," he grumbled.

"You don't have to stay there," Uncle Joe told him.

Larry brightened. Uncle Joe would speak to Miss Mills, and she'd have to promote him. Back on the mainland, parents were always visiting school and fixing things up for their kids.

"She'll move you along when you're ready," Uncle Joe went on. "You're a smart boy. If you put your mind to it, you'll be reading with the best of them in no time. It's up to you."

Larry knew better than to argue. Uncle Joe always meant what he said. The only way Larry was going to get out of the baby class was to earn his way out. And he would if it killed him, he decided.

The days of September flowed evenly along. Some were dim and mysterious with fog. Larry had never seen anything like the island fogs. They started as mile-high, sunlit walls standing out to sea. Then long streamers moved in over the island, dimming the sun. Soon the whole world was gray. The eaves dripped, the sparse grass was beaded with drops of moisture, and the nearest house disappeared behind the thick, soft curtain. Sounds seemed louder than before—the bark of a dog, the pounding of a hammer, the talking of men in invisible boats—and they came from wrong directions. It was eerie.

Some of the days were bright and golden. The maple trees behind the house blazed like crimson torches against the dark spruce and fir. One day the ferrymen brought reports of frost on the mainland. Islands, Uncle Joe told Larry, always had milder winters than the main. The surrounding sea kept the temperature more even.

"But when she blows!" Uncle Joe whistled. "Talk about gales! We invented them out here."

September was a good month for Larry. Miss Mills moved him to the middle reading class, for one thing. "You'll be in the top group soon," she predicted. "You're improving fast. Reading isn't so hard, is it?"

"Nope, not when you get the hang of it. It's sort of fun." Larry hadn't planned to say that, but once it was out, he realized that it was true. He did like to read.

For the first time in his life, he liked school. He knew that it was a funny little school, and he knew that he had to work harder at his lessons than ever before. With so few pupils, there was no chance that the teacher wouldn't notice if you were not prepared. But she always had time to explain things that you didn't understand. He'd learned more in this one month than in any three months back in the city.

Then one Saturday, when he was out hauling with Uncle Joe, he brought the *Petrel* into harbor all by himself. He kept expecting Uncle Joe to take over the wheel as usual when they entered the channel. Finally he looked over his shoulder to see what the trouble was. Uncle Joe simply motioned him to keep on, and continued cleaning up the deck. Larry felt a moment's panic. Then he slowed the *Petrel* and edged carefully in among the moored boats to their own buoy.

"Couldn't have done better myself," Uncle Joe commented.

"Whew!" Larry let out the breath that he hadn't

known he was holding. "I was scared for a minute there."

Uncle Joe grinned. "Figured you might be. That's why I didn't tell you what I had in mind. I knew you could do it, else I wouldn't have let you try. And you come through first-rate."

This was the biggest thing that had ever happened to him, Larry decided—bigger even than the time he had been chosen to play in the Little League finals. Baseball was only a game. Handling a lobster boat was for real.

Larry felt good all the way up the hill to the house. He and Uncle Joe found Aunt Emma bustling around the kitchen. She started talking almost before they were through the door.

"I was down to the store this morning and run into Lavinia and Minerva and some of the others. We were saying that we might not have many more good Saturdays like this, and we ought to take advantage. We thought a picnic would be nice. We haven't had a village picnic in dear knows when."

Uncle Joe heaved a mock sigh. "All right, what chores have you got lined up for Larry and me?"

Though he knew it wasn't true, Larry could almost believe that this picnic was planned especially to celebrate his first bringing in of the *Petrel* to harbor. "What do you want me to do?" he asked Aunt Emma eagerly.

"You can make up some bread-and-butter sandwiches. The butter's there on the table, softening up.

Pa, take that pan of eggs off the stove—they must be boiled hard by now. Just give me a little elbowroom, the both of you, while I get my cake out of the oven, and—"

Uncle Joe winked at Larry. "Ma missed her calling," he observed seriously. "She ought to be bossing a chain gang."

Aunt Emma refused to rise to the bait. "—and then," she went on as though Uncle Joe hadn't spoken, "you can get that big basket down from overhead in the woodshed, Larry. Pa, you bring up a couple of jars of pickles from down cellar—"

In spite of what seemed for a while like hopeless confusion, everything was ready by three o'clock, the time set for the picnic.

"We're having it at Schooner Head," Aunt Emma informed them. "That's just the right distance—far enough so you feel you've been somewhere, but not so far that you're all tuckered out getting there. Harvey Rice and old Perley Stevens are taking the lobsters and washboiler around by boat. All we've got to worry about is our own gear. You take the basket, Pa. Larry, you take this shopping bag. I'll carry the cake myself, to be on the safe side. Now let me make certain we've got everything—"

The path to Schooner Head left the road above the Chandlers' house and wound through the woods to the east side of the island. Already, people laden with baskets and blankets were straggling up the hill in an untidy procession. Uncle Joe went off with Horace Vance.

"Here come the other children," Aunt Emma said. "Go along, Larry—don't fret about me." A group of her friends called to her, and she joined them in a flurry of exclamations and laughter. "Don't swing that bag around careless now, Larry," she called back to him. "It's got breakables in it."

"I won't, Aunt Emma," he assured her, smiling. He was thinking that she looked younger and almost pretty, with her eyes sparkling and her cheeks pink with excitement. He fell into step with Tom, Sally, Linda, and Matt.

"If anybody enjoys a sociable, it's Aunt Em," Matt announced. He was smiling, too. "Picnic, sewing circle, church supper, makes no difference what, Aunt Emma's right to the forefront."

Larry's smile faded. Matt was at it again, mimicking him, slyly reminding him that Mrs. Chandler was not his aunt, that he had no aunts, that he was a State Kid. He'd had just about enough of Matt's smart-alecky jibes.

"Quit calling her Aunt Emma, Matt, will you?" he said. "I've got your message."

Matt turned to him with an air of innocence that Larry was sure was put on. "Why should I quit?"

"Because I say so, that's why, or how'd you like a poke in the nose?"

Sally started to laugh, then stopped when she saw

Larry's face. "Oh, for heaven's sake, Larry!" she exclaimed disgustedly. "She is his aunt, after all."

Larry couldn't believe it. "She is not. What do you know about it, anyhow? She isn't, is she, Linda?" Linda should know. She was born on the island.

Linda nodded. "Yes, she is. Most of us out here are related someway. I'm Matt's second cousin."

Larry had never felt so foolish in his life, and Matt was entirely to blame. Matt had planned to make him look silly—of that he was sure. "Why didn't you say so before?" he demanded angrily. "How was I supposed to know?"

"I thought everybody knew," Matt said.

"That's right," Tom interposed. "Come on, Larry, knock it off. It's not Matt's fault that you made a mistake."

"It's not important, anyhow," Sally added. "Don't make a federal case out of it."

Tom and Sally were right, of course, Larry knew. He knew he ought to laugh and then forget the whole thing. But he couldn't. There was just something about Matt that made him mad.

They came out of the woods onto Schooner Head. The great ledges that stepped down to the sea were bright and busy with people. A big fire was burning in a deep crevice in the rocks, and some of the men were collecting driftwood to feed it. The women were spreading blankets on the ground and unpacking picnic baskets. Two men were carrying a huge copper boiler

full of seawater to the fire. Others were catching the lobsters that Harvey Rice and old Perley Stevens tossed from the boat that was riding the gentle swells just offshore. The smaller children were scouring the ledges for big, clean scallop shells.

"These are to hold melted butter for the lobsters," little Tony informed Larry breathlessly. "Gee, Larry, isn't this fun?" He ran off to add his shells to the pile by the fire.

Tony's pleasure was contagious. Larry felt his spirits rise. He found Aunt Emma and delivered the shopping bag to her. Then he went down to the shore. He saw Mr. Vance drop a lobster into the sea and heard the good-natured jeers that went up. As an old Little League player, he himself could do better than that, he decided. He stepped in and neatly fielded the next lobster that came flying across the gap of water. The shout of approval completely restored his good humor.

After all the lobsters were safely ashore and cooking in the boiler, someone started a stone-skipping contest. All the men and boys hunted for small, flat stones to send hopping over the water. Bert Elder, the plump storekeeper, won. His third try skipped eleven times, a remarkable feat. He admitted that he was more surprised than anyone, and couldn't ever do it again.

Then one of the women called that the lobsters were done. Uncle Joe and Lon Cole lifted the boiler from the fire and emptied it on the rocks. Everyone snatched a lobster, tossing it gingerly from hand to hand to cool it. The scallop shells were filled with melted butter, the lobsters were cracked with stones, and for a while there was very little talking. Everything tasted so good there on the ledges in the salty air—the lobster, the deviled eggs, the sliced tomatoes and cucumbers, even the plain bread-and-butter sandwiches. All the women had brought pies and cakes, which were shared. Larry ate three kinds of pie and two kinds of cake. He didn't have room for more.

After the meal, everybody leaned back and relaxed on the ledges, still warm from the sun. Talk ran along quietly. The sun sank and a chill came into the air. The smaller children began to droop.

"Time we was starting home," Mrs. Albee announced. "Ethel here's half asleep on her feet."

"All right, fellers," Horace Vance said. "The womenfolk got up this picnic. It's up to us men to clean up. Look alive, everybody." He began to gather lobster shells, cardboard boxes, and pieces of paper, and toss them in the fire. All the men followed suit.

Larry picked up a leftover log and threw it onto the coals. Immediately Matt Cole snatched it off. "Just burn the trash," he said. "We always plan to leave some firewood for the start of the next picnic fire. Put this log over there under the lee of the ledge."

Larry turned on his heel. "Put it there yourself," he said over his shoulder. Matt wasn't going to boss him around. He picked up the empty washboiler and put it in the skiff, to be rowed out to Harvey Rice's boat.

"Hey," Matt called, "bring that boiler back. We ain't through with it yet. How do you think we're going to drown the fire? Carry water in our hands? You'd ought to know we can't go off and leave a fire burning."

Larry did know it. He'd learned that once when he'd been a Cub Scout for a short time, back on the main. But he'd forgotten. He left the boiler where it was and stalked off into the woods. He wasn't going to stick around and take orders from Matt Cole or anybody that looked like him.

This would have been a wonderful picnic, if it hadn't been for Matt picking on him with his "Aunt Emma" 's, and his "you-do-this" 's and "you-do-that," 's he thought as he stamped along the path toward home. Matt somehow always managed to spoil everything for him.

59

❦❦ CHAPTER 7

One afternoon in October, Larry came home from school to hear Miss Carr's voice issuing from the kitchen. He had forgotten that it was time for her visit.

"You know," she was saying, "that the Division of Child Welfare was doubtful about placing children out here on an island. You remember how hard you all had to work to convince them. It didn't seem wise for the children, or for you either."

"But you think now—?" Aunt Emma sounded anxious.

Miss Carr laughed. "I wish I felt as easy about all my cases. I keep thinking there must be a catch somewhere."

"I can't think what it would be," Uncle Joe told her. "Larry's a mite standoffish at times, but he's easing up gradual. He's a good boy."

Larry suddenly realized that he was standing stonestill, straining his ears. He was sneaking, the way he had done in the foster homes over on the main. Back

60

there, he'd had to do it. He'd had to know what people were thinking, so that he could be prepared for what they were going to do to him. He didn't have to sneak here. He could tell how Uncle Joe and Aunt Emma felt, without spying on them.

Besides, he couldn't imagine Uncle Joe creeping up on people to hear what they were saying. The very idea made him want to laugh out loud. He began putting his feet down hard and whistling for Mate. He was through with eavesdropping.

Miss Carr had come over on the regular ferry. It could not wait while she visited the eight foster homes and talked with Miss Mills. One of the lobstermen would have to take her back to the mainland. Uncle Joe volunteered to perform this service.

"Fine," Miss Carr said. "I've a few more people to see, but I shouldn't be long. I'll meet you at the landing in an hour?" She went off down the road.

"As long as you're going anyhow, there's a few things you can pick up for me in Stillport." Aunt Emma looked around for a pencil and paper. "They're out of yeast down to the store—Bert forgot to order it—and see if you can match a spool of thread to this sample of cloth, and I ought to have some—" She went on, talking mostly to herself.

Uncle Joe cocked an eye at Larry. "A few things, she says. You'd better come with me, else I'll be there half the night."

"Can I?" Larry was suddenly excited. It had been

a long time since he'd seen cars moving along paved streets, or walked the aisles of a real store. It would be wonderful to be in the thick of things again.

Mate followed them down the road when, armed with Aunt Emma's list, they went to meet Miss Carr. Mate loved boat rides and was always hopeful that he'd be invited to go on one.

"No," Uncle Joe said when Larry asked about taking the dog. "I've tried it and it don't work out. He's not used to traffic and crowds and all the confusion. Tie him in the boat, and he howls his fool head off. Take him ashore, and he's bound to get run over or lost. He'd best stay home where he's safe."

Miss Carr was waiting for them. To Larry's delight, Uncle Joe let him take the wheel of the *Petrel*. Larry hadn't wanted to ask, for fear he'd seem to be showing off. The truth was, he admitted to himself, that he did want to show off to Miss Carr. Uncle Joe didn't make a big thing of turning the boat over to Larry. He acted as though this were a commonplace. Trust Uncle Joe to understand.

Miss Carr was suitably impressed. "I can't believe that six weeks ago you'd never even seen a lobster boat. Look at you now—a regular old sea dog. You do like Star Island, don't you, Larry?"

Larry found himself telling her all about the island and his life there, about Mate, and school, and going out to haul with Uncle Joe. It wasn't until they had reached Stillport, and Uncle Joe had taken command in the unfamiliar waters, that he realized that Miss Carr had really been interviewing him.

Other times, when he had lived in mainland foster homes, she had asked questions and he had answered them as shortly as possible. She had once told him that getting information out of him was as hard as pulling hens' teeth. That was the way he wanted it. The less social workers and foster parents knew, the less they'd have to use against him.

Now he realized that Miss Carr was simply doing the job for which she was paid, and that nobody was trying to trap him. Maybe it had been that way all along. He couldn't help believing, though, that the island and the Chandlers were different from the other places and the other people.

When at last he and Uncle Joe stood on the main street of Stillport, Larry sympathized with Mate. There were people hurrying in all directions, and cars honking constantly. Although he had always been used to city traffic, Larry was almost afraid to cross the street. He had forgotten how big and fast automobiles were.

He followed Uncle Joe into a glittering supermarket. The sun was still shining brightly outdoors, but inside, lights glared overhead. When Uncle Joe inquired where they kept the yeast, the clerk never even looked at him. He said crisply, "Dairy case, further wall," and went on shelving packages. Bert Elder, on the island, would have stopped whatever he was doing, found the yeast himself in the shadowy cavern of his store, and then settled down for a long gossip.

It was the same in the other stores. The woman who matched the sample of cloth to a spool of thread wasn't even interested in what Aunt Emma was planning to sew. When Larry and Uncle Joe stopped at the drugstore for a snack, the soda jerk got Larry's order of a chocolate sundae right, but he put cream in Uncle Joe's coffee. Uncle Joe had said clearly that he wanted it black. The mainland wasn't the same as Larry remembered it, he could see.

The sun was setting when they finished their shopping.

"There, that's done," Uncle Joe said with relief. "An hour on the main tires me out more than hauling two hundred traps would. Let's head home, Larry."

Larry hesitated. Perhaps he didn't have the right to suggest this. "Could we maybe get something for Aunt Emma? Not the things she asked for, but a surprise?"

"That's a first-rate idea. Wish I'd thought of it myself. We'll get her a box of store candy. Bert don't carry nothing but candy bars. Claims he can't sell fancy chocolates. Ma really relishes a good box of candy."

The trip home was uneventful. The sea was a shimmering sheet of rose and gold in the glow of the sunset, with the lights of Stillport falling away behind and the dark loom of the island drawing nearer over the bow. When they entered the harbor, the windows

64

of the village were springing to life in the twilight—soft, golden squares climbing the hill.

It was good to be back, Larry thought, back to where he knew every single person by name. He could tell pretty nearly what was going on behind each one of those lighted windows, and he could walk up the rough road in the half-dark without once stumbling over an outcropping of ledge. He felt as though he had been gone for a long time.

"I'll put you ashore before I snug down the boat," Uncle Joe said. "You go on up and tell Ma she can get supper started. I'll be along directly. Here, take Ma's present. It was your idea, so you ought to get the credit."

Larry paused in the light from the store window to unbuckle the tops of his high boots and turn them down. That was the way all the island men wore their boots when ashore, sort of careless and dashing. Then he went on, practicing walking like a lobsterman, with long, easy strides. He'd bet that anyone who didn't know better would take him for a real born-and-bred islander. He hoped so, anyhow.

His thoughts were interrupted by the sound of barking. He looked up the road. There was still enough light for him to see Mate prancing excitedly around Matt Cole. Matt had a stick in his hand. As Larry watched, he threw it as far as he could. Mate dashed after it, snatched it up, and came racing joyfully back to Matt.

Larry was suddenly furious. "Mate!" he shouted. "Here, old feller. Come on here."

Matt turned, surprised. Mate hesitated, looking from one boy to the other. Then he dropped the stick and trotted toward Larry.

Matt whistled piercingly and clapped his hands. "Here, Mate!"

Again the dog stopped. The tip of his tail wagged uncertainly. If this was a game, he seemed to be saying, he'd be glad to play if he knew the rules.

"You leave my dog alone!" Larry shouted angrily, coming up to where Matt stood.

Matt simply stared at him, too astonished to speak.

"Come on home, Mate," Larry said more calmly.

Matt found his voice. "He isn't your dog," he said.

Larry hit him. He didn't know he was going to until he felt the satisfying sting of Matt's jaw against his knuckles. Then he hit him again, harder. He had been wanting to do this for a long time. Old high-and-mighty Matt with his know-it-all ways!

"Hey," Matt said feebly. Then he exploded into a tornado of flying fists. He wasn't used to fighting, Larry could tell at once. Half his blows failed to find a mark. Those that landed hurt, though. Matt had years of hauling traps behind him, and he was strong and muscular. Larry felt his nose flatten under a straight punch and was aware of the warm trickle of blood over his lip.

"What's going on here?" a stern voice demanded. A

66

hand fell on Larry's shoulder and pulled him away from his enemy. "Just you simmer down, the both of you." It was Uncle Joe, coming up from the harbor.

"He—he—" Larry sputtered.

"Never mind that now. You go on home, Matt. Larry, you come along with me." Larry wouldn't have believed that Uncle Joe could speak so coldly. "Where's Ma's candy?"

Larry had forgotten the present. He looked around frantically and saw it lying on the ground. "It got stepped on," he said in a small voice.

"Pick it up and bring it along."

"It's all squashed."

"I said, pick it up and bring it along."

Larry picked up the sorry object and trudged along after Uncle Joe. Matt had disappeared. Larry wished that he could disappear, too. He couldn't see Uncle Joe's face, but his back looked grim and forbidding. Even Mate thought so. He trailed along, head and tail drooping dejectedly. Larry told himself that he'd been bawled out for fighting before. It didn't hurt. All you had to do was listen and say, "Yessir." But before, it hadn't been Uncle Joe.

Aunt Emma's eyes widened when she caught sight of Larry. She opened her mouth to say something, glanced quickly at Uncle Joe, and closed it again. Then she busied herself at the stove. This was something for the menfolk to settle between themselves, her closed expression said.

"Wash your face," Uncle Joe ordered, "then sit down over there. We've got a few things to talk out."

Larry slid the ruined box of candy behind a stack of dishes on the drainboard. Maybe if Uncle Joe didn't see it, he'd forget about it, and Larry could dispose of it later. He simply couldn't hand Aunt Emma that disgusting mess. She had been too nice to him.

Then he caught sight of himself in the mirror over the sink. His nose was swollen and one of his eyes was puffed and rapidly turning black. He looked terrible. Splashing cold water over his features and combing his hair didn't help much. He delayed as long as he could, but finally he had to face Uncle Joe.

"Now, who and what started that catouse?" Uncle Joe asked.

Larry guessed that "catouse" meant "fight."

"He's always picking on me," he said. "Thinks he's so smart!"

Uncle Joe just looked at him, his face wooden. Larry's words hung in the air. After a minute they began to sound childish, even to him.

He started over again. "Well, I called Mate, and he called him back, and he said Mate wasn't my dog, and—" Larry's voice trailed into silence. Put into words, the whole thing sounded a little silly.

Then he continued desperately, "It wasn't just tonight. It's all the time. He's always showing off, making me feel— I don't know. I just don't like him."

"Now we get to the root of it," Uncle Joe said. "You don't like him. How long since? What did he do in the first place to get you down on him?"

"Since the first time I laid eyes on him," Larry said hotly. "He thinks he's a big wheel. I could tell by looking at him. He—"

Larry thought hard. He couldn't answer the second question. He couldn't think of a single really bad thing that Matt had done to him. "It's not what he *does*," he said finally. "It's the way he does it."

Aunt Emma snorted softly. Uncle Joe remained granite-faced. "The way I see it, you've never given yourself a chance to like him. Let me tell you something. Matt was real excited when he heard you were coming. He was looking forward to having boys his own age on the island. I know that for a fact. We islanders know pretty much all there is to know about each other, being so few and so close. But you—you were as prickly as a sea urchin—wouldn't let him get near you. Oh, I've noticed, though I haven't said anything. I figured you two would work it out yourselves. But when it comes to fighting—Well, it's time someone straightened you out."

He paused, thinking over what he was going to say. "It's like this. We don't fight each other on Star Island. We can't afford to. We depend on each other too much. Times come when we've got nobody but ourselves to call on. We've got to trust each other, and fighting don't lead to trust."

70

"But I don't *like*—"

"I'm not talking about liking. It ain't in us to love everybody equal. Some on this island I don't like as well as others. But I get along with them—same as you've got to get along with Matt."

"You mean I've got to start buddying up to him?"

"I mean you've got to start treating him ordinary civil and decent. We ain't never had trouble here— what they call juvenile delinquency over on the main. We ain't going to have it started by somebody living under my roof picking fights. You got that clear?"

"Yessir," Larry mumbled.

Uncle Joe looked at him sharply. "That come out easy. Now I want to hear you say it like you mean it."

"I do mean it, Uncle Joe. I'll get along with him. I will, honest." Larry found that he did mean it. If that was what Uncle Joe wanted, he'd do it.

"That's a starter, anyhow. It wouldn't surprise me if you ended up tolerating him—maybe even liking him. Time will tell." Uncle Joe rose to his feet. "One more thing. About Mate. Matt was right, you know. He ain't your dog. He belongs to the whole family. As long as you're a member in good standing, he's part yours." He grinned. "Which part'll you take? Head or tail?"

Larry was so relieved that he began to laugh, even though the joke wasn't very funny. His face hurt, but he kept on laughing. It was good to be friends with Uncle Joe again.

71

Uncle Joe clapped him on the shoulder. "Now I guess we can eat. I'm about famished. You begin dishing up supper, Ma. I've got an errand outside, but I'll be back in a shake."

As he passed the sink, Larry saw him slip the flattened and sticky chocolate box from its hiding place and conceal it under his jacket. He wasn't going to shame Larry by making him give it to Aunt Emma!

Uncle Joe was the most wonderful person in the world, Larry thought. He'd do anything for him—even be more than ordinary civil and decent to Matt Cole.

❦❦ CHAPTER 8

Larry awoke one morning to a chorus of twittering birds. He was used to the mewing of gulls, the croaking of ravens, and the harsh cawing of fish crows. They were as much a part of the island music as the pounding of the surf and the keening of the wind. The few songbirds that lived among the gale-twisted trees above the village were seldom seen and almost never heard. Something unusual must be going on. He jumped out of bed and went to the window.

At the end of Aunt Emma's garden, the rowan tree, bowed under its load of orange berries, was alive with feathered creatures. They fluttered among the branches, eating the fruit, chirping, fighting. Larry had never seen so many birds in one place in his life.

He threw on his clothes and raced down the stairs. "Did you see all the birds?" he demanded before he was through the kitchen door. "Where did they come from? There were never that many back in the woods."

"From the north," Uncle Joe told him. "Star Island

is smack in the middle of one of the big migratory lanes of North America. In spring and fall a stream of birds rushes right over us like—well, like a river. A bird professor that visited here one fall told us all about it."

Aunt Emma chuckled. "My land, I never saw a man more took up with his work than that one. He was all over the place, eyes shining, hair on end, taking notes and pictures. Called Star Island an ornithologist's paradise. That's the fancy name for them that make a business of watching birds."

"How long will they stay?" Larry asked.

"Two-three weeks—as long as the weather holds. Then they're off south." Uncle Joe started pulling on his boots. "When they go, we figure winter ain't far off. There's a lot to be done around here before snow flies, so we'd better get at it. First thing, I'll put the boat on the beach this afternoon when the tide serves right."

When Larry went down to the harbor after school, he found the *Petrel* drawn up above the waterline, along with several other boats. Uncle Joe was busy scraping the hull.

"Aren't we going to haul any more this year?" Larry asked.

"Lord love a duck, of course we are. Us lobstermen work the year round. The only difference is that it's a sight tougher in winter." Uncle Joe tapped a plank thoughtfully. "That'll have to be replaced,

unless I want to find myself looking up through ten fathoms of seawater some cold Tuesday. A boat takes a lot of punishment, come winter."

"Lobstermen, too?"

Uncle Joe laughed. "Oh, sure, but we're more durable. We grow our own replacements."

It was not only the boats that underwent a thorough overhauling, Larry found when he went out with Uncle Joe on Saturday. All the other gear was inspected carefully. Traps with weak spots were taken ashore to be repaired. Old lines were replaced with new pot warp, as the thin, strong nylon rope was called. Frayed trap heads were discarded for new ones. His boat and gear were the most important things in a lobsterman's life—aside from his family— Larry came to understand. Not only a man's livelihood, but sometimes his very life, depended on them. Naturally he took the best possible care of them.

Preparations for the winter to come were not confined to seagoing equipment. There was plenty to be done on the land. When Larry first came to the island, Aunt Emma had been busy every day picking and preserving blueberries and raspberries. Before that, he could tell by the shelves of shining glass jars in the cellar, she had gathered and canned other wild crops that the island offered. He read the neat lables: gooseberries, blackberries, crabapple jelly, dandelion greens, dock greens, fiddleheads, and goose grass. Fiddleheads, Aunt Emma told him, were the young, curled fronds of ferns, and goose grass was a low plant that grew just above the tide line.

"The leaves are shaped like a goose's tongue—long and pointed. It's the first crop of the spring." Aunt Emma regarded the shelves admiringly. "Ain't that a handsome sight? I do like to go into winter with a full preserve cupboard."

Larry looked at the jars, gleaming red, amber, purple, and various shades of green. They were indeed a handsome sight.

"There's still the cranberries to tackle," Aunt Emma went on. "If you've a mind to, you can help with the picking in your spare time."

Larry almost asked, "What spare time?" In the months since he had ridden the long road from the city to the coast with Miss Carr, he had learned that there was more to living on an island than eating raw clams and watching the horizon for sails.

"After that," Aunt Emma continued, "there's the garden to bed down, and the storm windows to put on, and the house to bank— Oh, I tell you, we've got to flax round if we're going to get everything snugged down before the freeze."

Larry thought at first that bedding down the garden was going to be easy. Aunt Emma pulled up the dead plants, and he carried them onto a ledge in back of the house and burned them. The bonfire was fun. He watched the smoke rise in the still air and pretended that he was a marooned sailor signaling to a passing

77

ship. He could make wonderful black puffs by throwing damp leaves onto the brightly burning stalks. Then he dug up the dahlia bulbs for storage in the frost-proof cellar, while Aunt Emma raked the beds into neatness.

"That's a good job done," he said when they had finished.

"Not quite," she corrected him. "We need a few wheelbarrow loads of rockweed to top it off. I'll come down to the shore with you, first trip, to show you. It has to be well rotted to do any good."

Larry knew rockweed. It was the coarse seaweed that grew on underwater ledges, and during storms washed up on the shore to rot. It smelled almost as bad as Uncle Joe's bait.

"What's it supposed to do?" he asked. He couldn't imagine that rubbery mess doing anything good for a garden.

"Keeps the cold away from roots and bulbs, and at the same time improves the soil. A mulch, I suppose real gardeners would call it. Over on the main they pay good money for fancy mulches, and there ain't a one of them can hold a candle to rockweed."

The next time he saw a pretty garden, Larry thought as he wheeled load after load of rockweed up the steep road, he'd appreciate it. Pretty gardens didn't just grow. A lot of work went into them.

The Chandlers chose a warm, windless afternoon to bank the house. Uncle Joe came in early from hauling, so that they would have plenty of time to finish before

dark. First they unrolled lengths of tar paper and laid it in the sun to soften, so that it would not tear in handling. Then, as Aunt Emma and Larry held it, Uncle Joe fastened it with strips of wood all around the foundations of the house. The lower edge that overlapped onto the ground was weighted down with flat stones.

"There," Aunt Emma said with satisfaction, when they were done, "that'll keep the breezes out. In winter, floors can get awful cold without banking. You know," she went on, "tar paper is a blessing. When I was a child, we used to bank the houses with rockweed. Hauled tons of it up from the shore every year. Now that was a chore, I can tell you."

Larry could well believe it.

"We'll go up back tomorrow and cut evergreen boughs to cover the paper," Uncle Joe said. "They ain't really necessary to keep us warm, but Ma always has her heart set on them."

"Yes, I do," Aunt Emma informed them vigorously. "Tar paper may be a blessing, but it ain't pretty. I take pride in my home, and I want it to look nice, summer *and* winter. And you do, too, Pa. You know you do."

Busy as everybody on the island was with the fall work, Larry had seen little of Matt outside of school. He had been a little apprehensive about meeting him on the day after the fight. He couldn't blame Matt if he wanted to finish the battle. What would he do if Matt hit him first? He'd have to hit back, and he didn't want to break his promise to Uncle Joe. He'd just have to try to keep out of Matt's way until things smoothed over.

As it turned out, Matt was as anxious to avoid trouble as Larry was. Probably his father had said much the same things as Uncle Joe had said. Matt, his jaw swollen, arrived at school almost late, and glanced at Larry's black eye. He almost smiled, and Larry felt a surge of anger. If he dared to laugh! But Matt quickly controlled his features. Miss Mills looked sharply from one boy to the other, but she said nothing.

The weather continued mild, one brilliant day following another. One evening Aunt Emma called excitedly for the others to come outside and watch the northern lights. Larry had never seen such a sight.

Long streamers of cold fire filled the whole sky like a huge battery of searchlights. They sank and rose, the colors changing constantly. It was mysterious and awesome.

The next morning, all the migrating birds were gone. The rowan tree, stripped of its berries, lifted empty branches to the sky. High in the blue, like a wavering wisp of smoke, a wedge of geese beat their way south through the thin, icy air. Their wild, sweet honking drifted down over the island, but there was no answering chorus of twittering. Larry had grown used to it, and now he missed it.

Uncle Joe was looking out the seaward window when Larry came into the kitchen. "It's a weather breeder," he said. "I'll move my shoal traps offshore today."

To Larry, it looked like any other day in the past two weeks, only maybe even nicer, and he said as much.

"Yup, too good to be true. When the main looks this near, and the nun buoy on Roaring Bull looms up so big, and you can hear the bell buoy on the Old Maid so clear, you can depend on it that dirty weather's brewing."

Larry joined Uncle Joe at the window. Sure enough, the mainland seemed to have moved closer, and the nun buoy looked near enough to reach out and touch. Even through the double windows, Larry could hear the measured clanging of the bell buoy as it swung on the lazy swells. There was not a cloud in the deep-blue bowl of the sky. It certainly didn't look as though it were going to storm, but Larry supposed that Uncle Joe knew what he was talking about.

"Better make me a mug-up," Uncle Joe told Aunt Emma. Larry had learned that a mug-up was a picnic lunch. "I'll be late, with traps to move. When it blows hard," Uncle Joe explained to Larry, "the traps in close are liable to wash ashore and smash up. A man can lose two-three hundred dollars' worth of gear. So when we smell a storm in the offing, we move them out into deep water or bring them ashore."

It was nearly sunset when Uncle Joe returned home. The sky had been dimming all day, and now thick, black clouds blotted out the last trace of blue. The sea was dark gray, laced with angry whitecaps. It churned and snarled over the offshore reefs, and ran, hissing, high on the island beaches.

"The wind's picking up," Uncle Joe said when he came in. His face was red with cold. "She's shifting round to the nor'east. Looks like we're in for it. I brought some extra flashlight batteries up from the store. We may need them before the night's over."

Lying in bed, later, Larry could hear the wind's muffled whooping over the roof, and the dull thunder of the surf on the backshore. A spate of rain like a handful of flung pebbles rattled against the window, and then a steady drumming sounded on the roof so close above his head. He snuggled down under the blankets. It was nice here in his little room under the low eaves, with Mate warm against his back and the storm howling outside—nice and cozy and safe.

He fell asleep.

❦❦ CHAPTER 9

Larry had no idea what time it was when he awoke. All he was aware of was noise. It seemed to come from everywhere—roaring, howling, pounding, crashing. Mate was no longer on the bed. Larry got up and went to the window.

The glass was streaming with wind-driven rain, but through it Larry could see blurred squares of light on the drenched earth below—reflections from the kitchen lamps. Uncle Joe must be up. Larry lifted his eyes. Instead of the darkness that usually shrouded the island at night, he saw lighted windows all the way down the road to the harbor. The harbor itself was blazing with light through the curtain of the rain. Each boat stood out against the blackness. Each was straining and tugging at its moorings like a frightened horse.

Where was all the light coming from? What was going on down there?

Then Larry remembered what Uncle Joe had said about the flashlights. Everybody on the island must be down there with a light, guarding the boats to see that none broke loose in the gale. Everybody except him! He tore into his clothes and took the stairs in three giant strides.

The clock on the shelf in the kitchen showed half-past two. Aunt Emma was alone there. "I didn't let Pa rouse you," she began. "A growing boy needs his sleep and—"

Larry wasn't listening. He was pulling on his boots and slicker. He whirled through the door and stopped short, gasping. It was as though he had stepped into the stream from a fire hose. The gale-force wind was driving the rain almost horizontally across the island. He caught his breath and, head bowed and shoulders hunched, fought his way down to the harbor.

He had been right. All the men of the village were there. They stood spaced along the shore, playing their powerful flashlights on the plunging vessels. The air was filled with flying spume. Great waves tumbled through the narrow channel into the little basin, fanning out and climbing higher and higher under the stilted wharves. Beyond the harbor entrance, Larry could see the tremendous surf in the reflected glow of the lights. The huge combers reared out of the blackness of the night, piling onto each others' backs. Their wild crests smoked as they raced toward the island, and the ground trembled as they crashed on the ledges.

Larry looked around for Uncle Joe. Everybody was wearing oilskins, and everybody looked alike in the unsteady light. Two smaller figures must be Matt and Tom, but he could not tell which was which.

Finally a voice spoke from behind him. "I didn't think Ma could keep you away long." It was Uncle Joe.

At that moment a shout went up from across the harbor. It was distorted by the wind and half drowned by the roar of the storm, but Uncle Joe seemed to understand.

"Here," he shouted over the tumult, thrusting the giant flashlight into Larry's hands. "Keep the beam trained on the *Petrel*. If she starts to drag anchor, put up a holler. They're in trouble over there and I got to—" Whatever else he said was lost as he began to run along the shore.

The *Petrel* was plunging and tossing, her bow alternately buried in foaming water and lifted high in the air. But she was not drifting from her mooring. The same was not true of the boat beyond her. It was moving with increasing speed toward the ledges. Each wave picked her up and flung her violently onward. Even Larry, inexperienced though he was, could see that unless something was done soon, her hull would be shattered on the rocks.

Something was being done. The little cluster of men that Uncle Joe had joined was launching a skiff and holding it steady while two of them climbed aboard. One perched on the bow and the other picked up the oars. Larry guessed that the one in the bow was the owner and that he would try to get aboard his boat. If he could start the engine in time, he could probably run her safely into deeper water and reset the anchor.

"Gee whillikers, did you ever see anything like this?" Tom had come up unseen and unheard. "Lot of gear going to be smashed up tonight." Tom was beginning to talk and think like a lobsterman, Larry noted. Well, so was he himself, for that matter. It was easy to fall into island ways.

He started to answer, and then he saw Mate. The dog was standing on the very end of one of the wharves. Although Larry could not hear him, he could see by the watery light that he was barking furiously. Just like the old fool, he reflected fondly. He thinks the storm will lie down and play dead just because he says so. He turned his eyes back to the *Petrel*.

The next time he glanced in Mate's direction, a wave greater than all the others was surging toward the wharf. Borne on its crest was a long pile, torn from some landing. As Larry watched, the wave flung it broadside against the underpinning of the wharf. The long stilts buckled under the terrific blow, the wharf tilted, and Mate began scrambling desperately on the slippery planking.

Then, before Larry's horrified eyes, he lost his footing and plunged into the churning water. The wave retreated with a harsh grumble of loose stones grinding against each other. Larry saw—or thought he saw— Mate's big black head amid the rubble of broken timbers that covered the water. Then it was gone.

Larry looked about frantically. Nobody else had seen what had happened. Everybody was watching either his own boat or the two men in the skiff. Panic washed over him. Mate was going to drown unless someone helped him. There'd be no joyful whining when Larry came home from school, no comforting warmth against his back at night. Mate had been his first friend on the island. Larry had to save him. There was no one else to do it. By the time he had explained, it would be too late.

He thrust the flashlight into Tom's hands. "Keep her trained on the *Petrel* and if she starts to drag anchor—"

"I know." Tom sounded impatient. "I've been here as long as you have."

Larry hadn't waited to hear. He was running to where Uncle Joe's skiff was drawn up. He had launched it many times, and he knew how to handle it. Just the other day, Uncle Joe had complimented him on his skill with a small boat. Even in this sea he should be able to rescue Mate.

The boat went into the water easily. Larry clambered aboard and picked up the oars. An ebbing wave carried him out before he had even started rowing.

With the first stroke he realized that he was in trouble. He could not even keep the bow into the sea, as he had been taught. In spite of his most strenuous efforts the boat drifted broadside away from where he had seen Mate. He observed with dismay that she was shipping water over the sides. Then, to his horror, he saw that he was being carried toward the jagged ledges that guarded the channel.

Too late he realized that he should never have attempted this rescue, that handling a boat in calm waters was far different from battling a heavy sea. With a sick, sinking feeling he knew that he was helpless to prevent the loss of the skiff, Uncle Joe's skiff of which he was so careful and so proud. It was going to be smashed to kindling wood on the rocks, and he, Larry, was entirely to blame.

There was a thud that jarred the boat. Probably a floating timber, Larry thought. Then a voice shouted in his ear, "Move over! Give me one of the oars! Now *row,* darn it, *row!*"

Vaguely Larry realized what had happened. Someone had jumped from a wharf into the boat. It must have been a long and chancy jump, and a dangerous one. But he didn't have time to think about that. He bent his back into the rowing, pulling until he thought his lungs would burst and his arms would be torn from their sockets.

After a long while he felt the grate of pebbles under the bow. The boat had stopped rolling and pitching and was firm on the harbor beach. Larry leaned on his oar, gasping. Then he raised his head and looked about him. The lights still played on the lobster boats, and the two men had reached the vessel that was dragging anchor. Everything—the wind, the rain, the watchful men—was just the same as it had been before he started on this stupid venture. That seemed hours ago, but it couldn't have been more than a few minutes. Nobody seemed to have noticed his absence. Nobody except his unknown rescuer.

He turned then to his companion. The words of gratitude died on his lips. It was Matt Cole.

Matt was resting on his oar, regarding Larry with level eyes. "That was a fool trick," he said. He sounded much older and wiser than Larry. He sounded almost like Uncle Joe.

"I know," Larry told him miserably. "But Mate was drowning and—" He started up wildly. "Now he's drowned!" Tears filled his eyes. "Now it's too late."

Matt said in his oddly adult manner, "Mate's fallen into worse seas than this plenty of times. It takes more than a hatful of water to drown an island dog. He was back on the beach bossing things before you got this boat into the water."

So, Larry thought, he'd almost wrecked Uncle Joe's boat for nothing. Only *almost*, thanks to Matt.

"Matt, I— Well, you could have drowned yourself, jumping like that. I—well, thanks." It came out hard, but he meant it.

Matt pulled inboard the oar he was holding, and stood up. "Better run this tub up on the beach out of harm's way." Then he looked down at Larry coldly. "You don't need to thank me. I didn't do it for you.

90

I'd have done as much for a stranger. Anybody would have. A man don't stand by and let a good boat founder. Everybody knows that." He climbed out of the boat and walked away.

Larry watched his retreating back. All right for him, if he wanted to be that way. Old smarty-pants Matt.

But underneath, he didn't blame Matt. Matt couldn't be expected to forget the way Larry had acted toward him, just for a simple "thank you." He had too much pride. Deep inside, Larry felt respect for the other boy growing—respect and something else that could have been the beginning of liking.

CHAPTER 10

After Thanksgiving, winter settled down over the island. One driving storm of mixed rain, sleet, and snow followed another. On the mainland these storms were mostly snow. From the island, after each of them, the main looked like a distant fairyland, glistening white in the sunshine between the dark-blue water and the bright-blue sky. It did not seem possible that ordinary people were going about their everyday business over there. So pure and lovely a place ought to be inhabited by elves or angels, Larry thought. He said something like this—although not quite, because it would sound sissified—to Aunt Emma and Uncle Joe.

"Depends on your point of view," Aunt Emma told him. "I've heard tell that from there after a snowstorm this island looks like a vision of the life to come—all alabaster and pearly gates and us sitting around in flowing white robes playing harps."

Uncle Joe laughed and reached for his boots. "That'll be the day. Not that I've got any special hankering to take up harp playing, even if I had the time. Which I ain't."

That was true. Even though the lobstermen went out to haul less often, sometimes only two or three times a week, there was plenty to do ashore. When stormy weather or dangerously ice-coated decks kept the boats in harbor, the men worked in their shops. Each had one, built at the end of his own wharf. The shops were alike, with windows facing the harbor, workbenches under the windows, and glowing potbellied stoves. The shops were filled with tools, coils of rope, spare engine parts, damaged gear, and bundles of laths for building new traps. They smelled of fish and of the sea, of tar and woodsmoke and freshly cut lumber.

Larry liked to go down to Uncle Joe's shop after school. There was always something he could do to help. He learned to build a good, stout trap, to varnish and sandpaper an oar until it felt like satin, to paint lobster buoys, to replace the broken handle of a boat-hook. It was pleasant in the shop, with the driftwood fire crackling in the stove, and the sound of water lapping on stone coming up through the floor.

Other men would drop in to borrow a tool or just to pass the time of day. They would talk of other days, and Larry would work quietly, listening with all his ears. He heard stories of storms and wrecks and ghost ships, of mysterious disappearances and buried pirate treasure. It was better than going to the movies had been, back on the main. These stories were true, or at

least partly true. It didn't cost anything to listen to them, either.

The question of money had suddenly begun to bother Larry. Up until now, he had not needed any, aside from the small allowance Uncle Joe gave him each week in return for the chores he did. Uncle Joe was not obliged to do this, but he insisted.

"A feller has to have a few coins to jingle in his pocket," Uncle Joe said. "It bolsters up his self-respect. You earn it. Not having to fill that tarnation woodbox myself is worth it to me, let alone the other chores you do."

"What'll I spend it on?" Larry asked. "I've got everything I want."

"Oh, supposing you wanted to buy a girl a candy bar, for instance."

Larry laughed. "What girl? Sally?" The idea was ridiculous. Sally, if he knew her as well as he thought he did, would manage to buy her own candy bars. As far as he was concerned, she could.

"Maybe. Or you might want to buy one for yourself."

So Larry accepted the allowance and tried his best to earn it. He found that Uncle Joe was right. It was a good feeling to have cash in his pocket, even if it wasn't much, and to be able to buy a bottle of pop or a comic book at the store if he felt like it.

Now, suddenly, everybody was thinking about Christmas. It started in school when Miss Mills put them all to work making cutout reindeer and Santa

95

Clauses to paste on the windows. She began talking about plans for a Christmas party, too, to be held on the last afternoon before vacation.

Then Aunt Emma sent over to the main for yarn for a sweater she was going to knit for Carl, and Uncle Joe spent an evening studying the mail-order catalog and making out an order that he wouldn't let Aunt Emma or Larry see. Christmas was coming, all right.

And Christmas meant gifts to give as well as to receive. Larry had not thought much about that until this year. Perhaps he had been too young before, or perhaps he had never cared enough about the people with whom he happened to be living to want to give them anything. Whoever they were, they had always had some little present for him, usually something useful, like a pair of socks. Even then, he had known that they gave it to him because they felt that they had to. They didn't want their own day spoiled by the sight of his forlorn face. He couldn't remember when he hadn't known that.

This year was different. He was pretty sure that Aunt Emma and Uncle Joe intended to give him presents, but that was not the point. Whether they did or not, he wanted to surprise each of them with something nice. They were not the same as the other foster parents had been. He really cared about them.

He knew exactly what he wanted to give them: a box of chocolates for Aunt Emma like the one that had been smashed in the fight with Matt, only twice as big; and a pair of sheepskin-lined slippers for Uncle Joe to wear around the house after the day's work was done. His old ones were shabby and down-at-heel. Larry knew, too, exactly how he could get these things without giving away his surprise. He could entrust the money to Miss Carr on her next visit and she would be willing to buy them on the main and send them to him by one of the ferrymen, he was sure. The crew of the ferry was always obliging about things like that.

There was just one difficulty. He did not have nearly enough money. Even if he saved every cent of his allowance for the next few weeks, he still would not have enough. If only he had some way of earning extra money!

Ever since he had come to the island he had watched Aunt Emma knit bait bags and trap heads, as did all the island women. They called it knitting, but it really wasn't. Instead of knitting needles, they used wooden shuttles that the men whittled for them. The women attached a length of strong twine to a window-sill, where the light was good. Then, as the shuttles flew in their nimble hands, a coarse netting grew into bags and heads. In every island kitchen one windowsill boasted a firmly driven nail, a shuttle, and balls of twine, all handy to be used when the mistress of the house had a free moment.

Larry had always considered knitting bait bags to be women's work. One noon while Aunt Emma was preparing dinner, Uncle Joe picked up her shuttle and finished three bags before she called the family to the table. All the men could knit and did, Uncle Joe told Larry, only usually they had other things to do. There was really nothing to it, he said. It was just a question of tying knots. Once you caught on to the trick, it was as easy as rolling off a log.

"It's getting to be a lost art, though," he concluded. "It used to be a disgrace if a man couldn't depend on his womenfolk to keep him supplied with heads and bait bags. Now a lot of the lobstermen over on the main have to buy theirs from the islanders. Their own women are gallivanting around or working in the sardine factories. They don't have the least idea how to make a bait bag."

"Don't fuss, Pa," Aunt Emma advised him. "I make a pretty penny over the winter months when I have time to knit extra bags to sell."

"How do you get them to market?" Larry asked. Aunt Emma seldom left the island.

"Jake Wise buys all I can make and sells them on the main." Jake Wise was the dealer who came once a week to collect the island lobsters from the storage tank floating in the harbor.

"Gee, do you suppose he'd buy them from me? That is, if I could learn to make them?"

"You could learn all right. You've got clever fingers," Aunt Emma assured him. "And Jake is always hollering for more bait bags."

So Larry found himself in business. A windowsill was set aside as his, and he invested part of his slim savings in twine. Jake Wise promised to buy all he could make. Aunt Emma told him that he could figure on clearing about ten cents on each bag. It took her about ten minutes to make one. It would take him longer, of course. Even so, he would be able to buy his gifts before Christmas.

Sitting in the kitchen with Aunt Emma after school was almost as much fun as being down at Uncle Joe's shop. The room smelled of gingerbread and cinnamon and of Aunt Emma's rose-scented geraniums. She was full of stories, too. She liked to tell Larry about life on the island when she was a girl.

"Every house on the island was busting at the seams with children, then. It took some scratching to make a living, I can tell you. Nothing come easy, like it does now. We raised all our own vegetables, and everybody had at least one cow and a big flock of hens and some sheep and a few pigs. We made all our own butter and smoked our own bacon and spun our own yarn. My, we were busy then!"

Larry did not see how anybody could be much busier than the islanders were now.

The Saturday after Miss Carr's December visit, Larry decided to take a holiday. Miss Carr had been glad to do his errands and had been pleased with him for his efforts. He was pretty pleased with himself, he admitted privately. He'd worked steadily and he deserved a day off. He hadn't taken Mate for a long walk in weeks. Mate enjoyed company on his rambles over the island. They'd start right after breakfast and go along the shore clear over to the back side, coming home through the woods. It would be fun.

It was just as much fun as Larry had anticipated. He saw raccoon and deer tracks in the light snow, and found a perfectly good lobster trap, which he carried above the tide line for later recovery. Mate chased rabbits and barked himself hoarse at the squirrels scolding the two walkers from the treetops.

It was when the two were on the homeward stretch through the woods that Larry heard chopping. It startled him. He had thought that there was no one anywhere around. He advanced cautiously and found himself gazing through the trees into a little sunken clearing that he had not known was there. It was full of black alder bushes, each one loaded with scarlet berries. They glowed like jewels against the dark evergreens. It was like discovering a secret treasure hoard, Larry thought.

Only it wasn't secret. Matt Cole was there, cutting off berry-heavy branches with a hatchet and tossing them into a pile. Mate bounded up to him, and Matt glanced up and saw Larry.

"Hi," he said. He wasn't exactly friendly, but neither was he looking for trouble.

"Hi." The least he could do was to meet Matt halfway, Larry decided. "What are you going to do with the berries?"

Matt grinned. "Ma's been took with Christmas spirit. She's making wreaths like all get-out. Claims she needs red berries to liven them up."

"Hey, that's not a bad idea. Maybe Aunt Emma—"

Then Larry had an even better idea. The fir boughs with which he and Uncle Joe had covered the tar-paper banking were pretty, like a giant wreath encircling the house. They'd be even prettier with scarlet berries thrust in among the branches.

"Do you care if I pick some, too?" After all, Matt had found the berries.

Matt looked amazed at the question. "Heck, I don't own them. They're just growing wild. I've got enough anyhow." He hesitated, then said with a rush, "You can borrow my hatchet, if you want, just so you return it when you're done with it."

"Gee, thanks." That really was decent of Matt, considering everything. "I'll make sure you get it back."

Matt handed over the tool, picked up his branches, and was gone.

Larry's idea developed as he worked. He wouldn't take the berries home right now. He'd hide them among the ledges in back of the house. Just before Christmas, he'd slip out after supper, when it was dark, and put them in place. Aunt Emma would be some old surprised when she saw them the next day.

He was so pleased with his plan that he told Matt

about it when he stopped at the Coles' house to return the hatchet. "Don't tell anyone," he requested. "I don't want it to get back to Aunt Emma and spoil the surprise."

Matt grinned. "I won't tell a soul. I'd sure like to see her face, though, when she catches sight of them."

"It'll be worth seeing," Larry agreed. Then, without thinking, he found himself saying cheerfully, "So long. See you around."

Matt responded just as cheerfully. He might not be so hard to get along with, once you got to know him, Larry thought as he made his way up the hill toward home.

❧❧ CHAPTER 11

School closed for the midwinter vacation on the Friday before Christmas. The party was held in the afternoon, and everybody on the island attended. As Uncle Joe said when Larry invited the Chandlers, "We don't have so many sociables out here that we can afford to miss one. We'll be there."

"I'll make some cookies for you to take," Aunt Emma volunteered. "I know you haven't asked me yet, but you were about to. I've had young ones in school, and I know the ropes."

Larry thanked her. All the children were bringing something good to eat, and Miss Mills was contributing soda pop from the store. They had all agreed that a party must have refreshments.

It was a good party. Miss Mills welcomed the guests for all of them. Then the pupils presented a Christmas program. Everybody had a part, and nobody forgot his lines. The applause was enthusiastic. This was followed by a community sing of Christmas carols, with the deep, rumbling voices of the fishermen supporting the clear trebles of the smaller children. The little building seemed to bulge with song.

Finally it was time for refreshments. Miss Mills had made it very clear that none of her pupils was to taste as much as a single cake crumb until all the guests had been served. There was a great deal of running back and forth with paper plates and cups. Everybody remarked on what good little hosts the children were. Miss Mills looked pleased with them all.

Then, from a place near a window, someone called that the ferry was in sight. This signaled the end of the party. The men had to be down at the wharf to help unload, and Miss Mills was going back to the mainland to spend the holidays with her family. People were starting to put on their jackets and caps when Horace Vance, the chairman of the school committee, tapped on Miss Mills's bell for attention.

"I'm not going to spoil this shindig by making a long speech," he said, "but I'd like to compliment Miss Mills on the job she's doing here. I know you all agree with me."

Everybody clapped, and Miss Mills turned pink with pleasure.

When the room was quiet again, Mr. Vance went on, "This is Christmas. Let's not forget to be thankful for a present we all share. I mean this school. You all know that we almost didn't have a school on Star Island this year. The town couldn't support one without state aid, and the state wouldn't give aid to a school with only three pupils. That would have meant that three of our families would have had to move to the main. They didn't want to go, and we didn't want to lose them. Good neighbors are hard come by."

He paused and then went on, "Luckily, we didn't have to lose them. The Child Welfare Division finally agreed to place eight foster children on the island, so that we could keep our school. When summer comes—"

"Sorry to interrupt, Horace," a voice called from the back of the room, "but the ferry's coming into harbor. We'd better hustle ourselves down there."

There was a little laughter, a little applause for the speech, and then everybody was streaming out the door and down to the shore.

Larry found himself standing in front of the building with Tom and Sally. The words "when summer comes" rang in his ears. He felt stunned and a little sick. He'd really believed that Uncle Joe and Aunt Emma had taken him in because they wanted him. Aunt Emma had even said it was good to have a boy in the house again. All the time, they had been just like all the other foster parents. They had used him to serve their own purpose, to keep their precious island the way they wanted it to be. He should have known. Things had been too good to be true all along. When summer came, Horry was going to say, they would be rid of the State Kids.

Tom's voice broke into his thoughts. "Now we know

why they wanted so many of us at once." He did not sound disturbed. He simply sounded rather pleased at finding the answer to a riddle.

Sally heaved an exaggerated sigh. "What a relief! You know what I thought? I thought maybe they were all mad scientists in disguise out here, and they were going to fatten us up and then perform experiments on us, like changing us into sea monsters or something. You know, like you see on TV. I thought probably that's really what became of their own kids, no matter what they said."

Tom hooted. "You really didn't believe that!"

"Well, maybe not *really*, but it was an interesting idea." Sally looked at Larry. "Hey, what's the matter with you?"

Larry hadn't expected Tom to feel as he did. Tom was new at being a State Kid. He hadn't learned what to expect. But Sally ought to understand. Her whole life had been like his own—one foster home after another ever since she could remember, one excuse after another for being shoved along when she was no longer needed.

"They don't care anything at all about us, that's what's the matter with me, if you want to know," he burst out. "All they care about is their darned old island and keeping it the way it was in the olden days. Aunt Emma herself said when we first came that Starhaven would end up as a ghost town unless something was done." He kicked a lump of ice viciously.

"What do you care *why* we're here?" Sally asked. "We're here. They take good care of us. You like it here—you said you did. So why don't you just relax and make the most of a good thing?"

"Because that isn't enough," Larry began heatedly. "I want—" Oh, what was the use of trying to explain! "I'll tell you one thing," he added. "We can plan on being shipped out as soon as school closes. They won't need us then, so why should they put up with us all summer? They can get new kids in the fall."

"You're crazy," Sally told him flatly. "People out here aren't like that. I'm smart about people and money, remember?" Her manner changed. "Come on, you two. Everyone's down at the ferry seeing Miss Mills off. We'll be too late if we don't hurry. She's a good egg, for a teacher. I want to wish her Merry Christmas."

She started running down the hill, red braids and long legs flying. Tom hurried after her.

Larry turned on his heel and walked up the road. He didn't stop at the house, because Aunt Emma and Uncle Joe would be home soon. He did not want to see them right now. He whistled for Mate, who came bounding from in back of the shed. Mate was his friend. He wasn't always scheming to get something. Mate liked him for himself. He was the only one in the world who did.

After Larry had walked in the wintry woods for a while, he felt a little better. The shock and hurt began to wear off. Besides, it was hard to feel gloomy and sorry for himself in Mate's company. Mate was so interested and enthusiastic about everything he saw. He called Larry's attention to rabbit tracks and little slate-colored juncos flitting through the underbrush. The woods were peaceful and quiet. The distant thunder of the surf drifting through the trees drowned the echo of the words "when summer comes." Larry wished he could stay there forever, with only Mate for company.

He thought about what Sally had said. For all she was a girl, Sally was tough and sensible. He'd try to take her advice, to make the most of a good thing, to enjoy the island while he could, and worry about the future when it came. If Sally could do it, he should be able to.

At least he had one advantage in this foster home. This time he knew where he stood. In spite of what Sally believed, he knew that all the State Kids would be sent back to the mainland as soon as school was over for the summer. Knowing, even if you didn't like what you knew, was better than wondering and hoping.

He turned his steps toward the village. He was ready now to face Uncle Joe and Aunt Emma. He'd have to pretend that things were the same, hard as that would be. But he had a whole lifetime of pretending behind him, of acting as though everything was fine when it wasn't. He could keep it up, he supposed. He'd have to.

He could smell the woodsmoke from the chimney

of the house when suddenly he stumbled over the pile of berry branches that he had hidden only last week. For a moment he felt hurt all over again, remembering how happy he had been. Then his hurt turned to anger. He'd try to act natural. He'd do all the things that were expected of him, just as usual. He'd even laugh and joke. But he'd be darned if he was going to arrange surprises. The heck with it.

He started kicking the branches wildly in all directions. Mate barked frantically, thinking it was a game.

"Hey! What's eating you?" It was Matt's voice.

"Where'd you come from?" Larry demanded roughly.

"I heard Mate barking and thought maybe he'd treed a squirrel. What's the big idea, kicking those berries around? Are you mad at Aunt Em about something?"

"Yes, I'm mad at Aunt Emma about something. What's it to you?" Larry's tone invited a quarrel, but he didn't care. He felt just like fighting someone.

But Matt only said comfortably, "You'll get over it. Come on, simmer down." Matt was sounding just like Uncle Joe again. "Look, why don't I meet you here after supper? The two of us can lug these branches down and get things fixed up in no time. How about it?"

If he refused, Larry thought, Matt would only argue. Anyhow, he'd decided to pretend that everything was all right, and this was as good a time to start as any. "All right," he agreed, and added grudgingly, "Thanks, Matt."

Matt grinned widely. "That's okay. Anything for a pal." He vanished into the woods.

Larry turned slowly homeward. A pal, Matt had said. They could have been pals, if Larry hadn't been so pigheaded. He'd been wrong about Matt. He'd wasted all the months when they could have been friends. Now it was too late. He'd probably never see Matt again after June. There was no sense in forming a friendship, unless it had a chance of lasting. It hurt too much when it ended.

❧❧ CHAPTER 12

At times during the long vacation, Larry had to remind himself that the Chandlers were just like all other foster parents. He had become so used to thinking of Starhaven as the place where he belonged that it was hard to remember the truth. He found himself believing that Uncle Joe really depended on him to help down at the shop, and that Aunt Emma meant it when she said that she didn't know what she'd do without him. It would be so easy to trust them again that sometimes he almost did.

Then he hardened his heart. He'd trusted foster parents before and what had it got him? Nothing but disappointment and grief. He was a State Kid, and he'd better not forget it.

He almost forgot it on Christmas, though. Aunt Emma said that it wouldn't have been much of a Christmas without her own children there, except for Larry. She kissed him when she saw the red berries around the house; and she almost cried when she opened his present to her. Uncle Joe smiled all over when he saw his new slippers. He threw his old ones into the stove and wore his new ones around all morning. Aunt Emma gave Larry a sweater that she had knit secretly while he was in school, and Uncle Joe gave him a jackknife with seven different blades. It took Larry's breath away. He had never expected to have a knife like this of his own. Surely the Chandlers wouldn't do all that for someone whom they planned to send away. Maybe Sally was right, after all. Maybe the people on Star Island were different.

Maybe, but he'd better not depend on it. Very likely they were sorry for what they were planning to do to him. Very likely they felt guilty. If so, he had a good thing going, and he'd better take Sally's advice and make the most of it.

Larry was so mixed up that he didn't know how to act. Sometimes he talked too much in a voice that didn't sound like his own. Sometimes he hardly answered when Uncle Joe or Aunt Emma spoke to him. He knew that the Chandlers were puzzled. He caught Aunt Emma watching him with a slight frown on her usually pleasant face. Once she placed a cool hand on his forehead and shook her head slightly. He didn't have a temperature, her manner said.

One night Larry heard Uncle Joe and Aunt Emma talking down in the kitchen after he had gone to bed. His name was mentioned. He crept to the head of the stairs and listened. He hadn't eavesdropped since his first month on the island. He hadn't thought it was necessary. Now he wasn't so sure. He had to know what was going on, and this seemed to be the only way of finding out.

But all he heard was Aunt Emma saying, "That boy's coming down with something. Maybe we ought to take him over to the main to see a doctor tomorrow."

Uncle Joe reassured her. "All that ails him is growing pains. He'll get over them, give him time." Then they talked about something else.

Matt added to Larry's confusion. He seemed to have forgotten their earlier difficulties. He showed up at the Chandlers' every morning, full of vacation plans for the day. They'd go over on the back side and look for good driftwood; or they'd dig a mess of clams; or they'd walk down to the harbor and see what was going on there.

The trouble was that Larry wanted to do all these things. He had a good time with Matt. But he had decided that a close friendship was foolish, and he meant to stick to his decision. That way, neither of them would be hurt.

So Larry made excuses. He had to help Uncle Joe, or Jake Wise was counting on him for bait bags. Matt accepted his excuses cheerfully and went off to find Tom. Larry was left alone and forlorn. It helped a little, but not much, to know that he had been Matt's first choice. Larry was glad, those times, that he had learned to like to read. Carl's books, on the shelves in his room, helped him through many a lonely hour.

It was easier after New Year's Day, when school started. In school, Larry could forget how things were at home. Miss Mills had come back from the mainland full of new ideas. She kept her pupils busy. Larry was glad of that, though he had to smile a little sourly at himself. He had never thought he'd be grateful for schoolwork.

February was stormy. One gale followed another, and the crystal days in between were bitterly cold. Sometimes the thermometer did not rise much above zero all day long. The lobstermen thought themselves lucky if they could get out to haul once a week. The rest of the time, high seas or iced-over decks kept them in harbor.

The first day of March began as a lovely day. The sun shone bright and warm, and the eaves dripped with melting snow even before Larry went to school. Uncle Joe was long gone. All the lobstermen were taking advantage of the fine morning.

Aunt Emma said, "March is coming in like a lamb this year," and went out to poke around her garden. She came back to report that her daffodils were up an inch under the rockweed mulch. "No use uncovering them yet, though," she said. "This weather won't hold."

She was right. When Larry went home at noon for dinner, the sky was overcast—smurred up, as the lobstermen said. The sound of the bell buoy was loud and demanding. The wind had veered into the north-

114

east, a bad quarter, and the thermometer was dropping. As he walked back down the road to school, Larry felt against his face the first hard, stinging pellets of snow that foretell a big storm.

All afternoon, as he sat at his desk and listened to Miss Mills, Larry had one ear cocked. The windows were white squares of blowing snow and fog, through which nothing could be seen, but the roar of the engines of returning boats sounded clearly from the harbor. He heard the first one during geography. It wasn't Uncle Joe. When Larry first came to the island, he had been amazed at the ease with which Aunt Emma could pick out the sound of the *Petrel's* motor from the others. Now Larry could do it himself, although he didn't know when he had learned.

Several boats came in during reading. Finally, during spelling, a familiar, deep-throated throbbing told him that Uncle Joe was safe ashore. He relaxed. He'd been foolish to worry. Uncle Joe knew his way around.

Dark came early that night. Aunt Emma had the kitchen lamps lighted when Larry got home from school. She was busy darning socks. Uncle Joe was not there. He hadn't come up from the harbor yet, Aunt Emma said. "Probably down at the store gossiping with the other men. Talk about women gossiping! They can't hold a candle to men. He'll be home when he gets hungry."

An hour later, when supper was ready and waiting, Uncle Joe still had not come. "I'd call the store on the walkie-talkie and tell Bert to send him home," Aunt Emma said, "except I don't hold with women interfering with their menfolk. But if he don't come in the next ten minutes—"

Just then they heard Uncle Joe outside the door, stamping the snow off his feet. He came in on a gust of cold air. His face was grim and troubled.

"What's happened?" Aunt Emma asked anxiously.

"Lon Cole ain't in yet."

Aunt Emma drew a quick breath. "Oh, poor Minerva!" Minerva was Mrs. Cole, Matt's mother.

"Lem Rice saw him around noontime away-and-gone beyond Egg Rock. He was all right then. Icing up some, but no more than natural. Then the snow closed in, and nobody's set eyes on him since—nor heard a peep out of him. His shortwave was out of

116

kilter, and he took it over to the main last week to be fixed."

Larry thought of Matt. It must be terrible for him, knowing that his father was alone out there somewhere in the blizzard. The sea was so big, and a lobster boat was so small.

"Isn't anybody doing anything about it?" Larry demanded.

"There ain't anything anybody can do until morning," Uncle Joe said heavily. "It's as black as the inside of your pocket out there, and blowing a full gale. It would be a useless risk of life to put out in search of him now. The Coast Guard's been notified, and they're on the lookout for him. They'll send a plane over in the morning, if the storm clears. And storm or no storm, come daylight the rest of us will go out. In the meantime—" His voice trailed off.

"Lon's a good seaman," Aunt Emma ventured almost timidly. "He'll ride it out, if anyone can."

"Sure he will," Uncle Joe told her with an attempt at heartiness. "Like as not we'll find him snugged down in the lee of some island, safe as houses."

"Can I go with you tomorrow?" Larry asked. He couldn't just sit around on dry land while everyone else was out looking for Matt's father. He'd go crazy.

Uncle Joe considered him thoughtfully. "I don't know why not. You're a good hand in a boat, and two pairs of eyes are better than one. Yes, you can go."

Aunt Emma began, "Oh, Pa, do you think you ought

to—" Then she stopped. She was remembering, perhaps, that island women didn't interfere in men's
affairs. "You'd better eat your supper, Larry, and then
go to bed. If you're going with Pa, you'll need a good
night's sleep."

When Larry looked out of his window, the last
thing he did before getting into bed, the snow was still
falling. Very dimly, through the blowing veil, he saw
a faint glimmer of light halfway down the hill.

That would be the Coles' house, he thought. There
would be little sleep under that roof tonight. Of that
he was positive.

❦❦ CHAPTER 13

By morning the storm was over. There were stars in the sky when Larry and Uncle Joe made their way down to the harbor. The east was faintly flushed with pink. The seas were very high, their thunder filling the air. It was cold. The rocks along the channel were sheeted with ice.

Every man on the island, bundled in heavy clothes and shrouded in oilskins, was preparing to go out and search for the missing boat. Larry saw Tom with his foster father and Matt with his uncle, Vince Cole. Bert Elder, the storekeeper and the only man on the island who never went to sea, was going today. Larry saw him with Horace Vance. Even old Perley Stevens, who was crippled with arthritis and had sold his boat and retired from the sea years before, was there.

Larry did not think that either Perley or Bert would be much help, and he said so to Uncle Joe.

"Bert's got good eyesight, and old Perley's got a lot stored in his head that could come in handy. He

119

knows every current and cross rip between here and Spain," Uncle Joe explained. "Out here on Star, we all stick together. Nobody knows but what he'll be the next one in trouble. At a time like that, it's a comfort to know that the whole island's out looking for you."

There was a droning overhead, and Larry looked up to see a small plane winging over the island. The sun shone on it, although the earth was still in shadow.

"Coast Guard," Uncle Joe said. "Well, let's get going. The sooner we start, the sooner we'll find Lon. He must be some old cold and miserable by now."

Larry didn't know whether Uncle Joe was as sure as he sounded that Lon was still afloat and alive.

Larry was even less sure himself, once they were clear of the channel and on the open sea. The waves had looked big enough from the shore. Out here, they looked like mountains. They picked the *Petrel* up as though she were a chip, carried her along, and dropped her into the deep troughs. Down there it was impossible to see anything but steep slopes of water. It wasn't much better up on the crests. The air was full of flying spume, and the familiar reefs and ledges all looked alike under the piling green combers. To Larry, the whole search seemed hopeless before it began.

Uncle Joe did not appear discouraged. His face was serious, but not dismayed. "We made our plans last night," he shouted over the noise of the engine and the sea. "Our section is from Egg Rock to the sou'west.

120

We'll go out to the Rock and then tack over toward the main. Keep your eyes peeled."

Larry nodded, and almost at once shouted and pointed to a floating object. Uncle Joe turned the bow of the *Petrel* toward it. It proved to be only a large tree trunk torn from some island by the storm.

"Never mind," Uncle Joe said. "We can't afford to overlook a thing. If Lon's boat broke up, there'd be wreckage afloat, and at least we'd know—"

He didn't have to say what they'd know. After that, Larry dreaded approaching any piece of driftwood that they spotted. He was relieved when each turned out to be meaningless.

After the sun came up, the visibility was much better. Larry could see the other boats now, twenty of them fanning out according to a well-laid plan. Off toward the horizon was the sleek gray Coast Guard cutter, and the Coast Guard amphibian circled overhead.

For the first time, he began to feel that there was a chance of finding Matt's father. Except for Tom and himself, everyone engaged in the search had been on this same errand before. They all knew what to do. He saw now what Uncle Joe had meant when he said that it would be a comfort, if you were lost, to know that the whole island was out looking for you.

It was about noon when the shortwave began to crackle. It had been agreed that silence should be kept except for urgent messages. Uncle Joe flipped the switch, gave his call number, and said, "Over."

It was the Coast Guard cutter, relaying a message from the spotting plane. What appeared to be a boat had been sighted aground on the northeast shore of Three Tree Island. The craft nearest the vicinity would please investigate. "Acknowledge," ordered the crisp voice of the Coast Guardsman. "Over."

"I read you," Uncle Joe said into the transmitter. He repeated the message. "I'm nearest of anybody, I reckon. I'm on my way. Over and out." He spun the wheel of the *Petrel* and pulled open the throttle. The boat leaned dangerously, then straightened and leaped forward. "Hold your hat," Uncle Joe advised Larry. "We're going straight out."

Probably Three Tree Island had once boasted three trees. Now it was barren and desolate. The seas broke heavily on the windward side, almost burying it in a smother of foam. It did not seem possible that anything could survive the constant battering.

Yet, when the *Petrel* skirted the island and came around to the sheltered side, there was a boat. Her bow was high on the cobblestone shore of a small cove, and her stern was awash with green seawater. She was encased in a thick coating of ice. There was no sign of life aboard her.

"That's Lon's boat, all right," Uncle Joe announced. "We'll run in as snug as we can and give a hail. If he's aboard—" His tone was calm and matter-of-fact, but

122

Larry could tell by the set of his lean face that he was facing the grim possibility of an empty boat. "No sense in getting on the shortwave and stirring folks up till we know what's what."

He throttled down the engine and started maneuvering into the little cove. It was fairly calm there, out of reach of wind and wave. "If we're lucky," Uncle Joe said, more to himself than to Larry, "the shore will drop off fast here and we'll have plenty of water under us. That way, we can get in close. . . . All right, Larry. Holler your lungs out."

He raised his own voice in a deep bellow, and Larry joined in as loudly as he could. Just as his breath gave out and he began to see spots before his eyes, Uncle Joe raised a hand for silence. Miraculously, above the noise of the surf and the wind, they heard a faint cry, and then a hammering sound.

Uncle Joe performed a little dance step on feet clumsy with cold. His face broke into a wide grin. Only then did Larry fully realize how worried he had been. "By golly," Uncle Joe crowed, "he's alive and kicking! From the clatter he's making, he's iced into the cabin. We better spread the good word before we start figuring on how to get him out."

It took only a moment to convey the news to the other boats. Uncle Joe turned off the radio in the middle of the questions that followed. There would be plenty of time to hash things over later, he told Larry.

Right now they had more important business to attend to.

"You take the wheel and ease her in," he instructed. "When I jump, back her off and hold her steady. We've got to do this alone. There ain't room for another boat in this cove, even if one was handy. Just take it easy, Larry. It's a little tricky, but it ain't dangerous. The worst thing that can happen is for me to lose my footing and take a dousing. But I been wet before, and it ain't never proved fatal."

He climbed onto the bow of the boat, moving slowly and carefully on the slippery surface. Larry gripped the wheel tensely. He had to do this right. Uncle Joe made light of the chance of falling into the icy water, but they were a long, cold way from home, dry clothes, and a warm fire. Uncle Joe was wonderful, but he could catch pneumonia like anybody else.

The whole thing was over before Larry had time to worry much. He saw Uncle Joe gather himself together and leap like a cat, in spite of his heavy clothing and clumsy boots, into the cockpit of Lon's boat. As Larry backed the *Petrel* away, Uncle Joe attacked the cabin door with his fists and feet.

The thick coating of ice starred, splintered, and fell away, and the door burst open. Lon Cole, blinking in the sudden sunlight, crawled out onto the deck. Uncle Joe said something to him, and to Larry's utter surprise, both men began to laugh.

Back on the mainland, Larry had seen plenty of

rescues on television and in the movies—rescues from the sea, from caved-in mines, from burning buildings. and from mountain precipices. There, the people involved always shook hands and made speeches. Sometimes they even cried. Larry hadn't expected that of Uncle Joe and Lon, but he certainly hadn't expected them to act as if they just happened to meet here. Island people certainly were different in more ways than one.

Uncle Joe waved a beckoning arm, and Larry guided the *Petrel* alongside Lon's boat. The two men scrambled aboard and Uncle Joe took the wheel. "We'll come back and tow Lon's boat off, the next calm day. His engine conked out in the storm. Serves him right for not taking care of his gear."

Larry knew that Lon took excellent care of everything that belonged to him, so he stared at Uncle Joe in amazement. Then Lon said, face straight, "Yup, I should have known better than patch her up with bobby pins and scotch tape," and Larry realized that they were joking.

"No sense lallygagging around here all day," Uncle Joe said cheerfully. "Let's head for home."

Word had gone ahead over the shortwave, so that everyone left in Starhaven was down at the landing when they came into harbor. Sally fell into step with Larry as he started up the hill.

"Did you know there wasn't even any school today? Everyone was too upset," she told him. "Gee, it must have been exciting out there, rescuing people and all. What happened? Tell me all about it." She was dancing with impatience.

For a moment Larry was tempted. He could really make her eyes pop out with a tale of gigantic waves, deadly reefs, and getting to Lon in the nick of time, just as his boat was about to break up. With only a little embroidery, he could make himself a hero. Then he remembered Lon and Uncle Joe laughing and joking at Three Tree Island.

"Nothing to tell," he said. "Nothing happened. It was part of a day's work, that's all."

Sally stopped short. "Oh, cut it out. You make me sick. You sound just like a darned islander."

"Sure I do. That's what I am." The words came out without thought.

Then Larry turned away quickly. For a while he had forgotten. He wasn't an islander and he never would be. After June, he'd probably never see the island again.

CHAPTER 14

Spring came fast to Star Island. It seemed to Larry that one day he was sprinkling rock salt on the kitchen doorstep to melt the ice from it, and the next he was helping Uncle Joe and Aunt Emma remove the banking from the house and the mulch from the garden. And the day after that, or so it seemed to him, golden daffodils were blowing and dancing against the stone foundations, and the migrating birds were back.

The children began counting the days before summer vacation began. Each time they drew a line through one of the squares on the calendar, Larry's heart sank lower. Everybody else was looking forward to the end of school. They were full of plans for the summer. When Larry heard them talking of picnics and tree houses and the possibility of catching baby seals to tame, he wondered how they could be so blind. Didn't they remember Horry's words, "when summer comes"? He didn't expect the little children to understand, but the others surely ought to realize that their days on the island were numbered. For the first time in his life he wanted school to go on forever.

One Saturday in late May, Aunt Emma announced at breakfast that she wanted to go to Stillport that afternoon. "So you plan to get in from hauling in good season, Pa," she directed. "We've got a lot of errands to do. Larry's sneakers are a disgrace, and—"

"Do I have to go?" Larry asked in alarm. He didn't want to waste a minute of his remaining time on the island.

"Yes, you do," Aunt Emma said flatly. "I can't buy you clothes without your trying them on. Besides, I should think you'd like to see something different for a change. Land, when my young ones had a chance to get over on the main, there was no holding them. You'd think they'd been offered a glimpse of Paradise."

Some Paradise, Larry thought. Maybe the mainland was a treat to kids who hadn't spent all their lives there, but it was no treat for him. He didn't want to go, and that was that.

"And you can take that look off your face," Aunt Emma continued, "because it won't do you any good. You're coming with us."

Aunt Emma had never spoken to him that way before, and Uncle Joe chuckled. "I ain't heard Ma use that tone of voice since Carl and Martha were your age. Takes me back to the old days. You're licked, boy, so you might as well give in graceful."

Stillport was even worse than Larry had expected.

There were too many cars and too many people. Everybody seemed worried and cross and in a hurry. The streets looked dirty and the air smelled of gasoline fumes, and greasy cooking from the restaurants. Larry didn't see how people could stand living there.

Soon, though, he would be living in just such a place. Not in Stillport, probably, and maybe not in a city. But that wouldn't make any difference in how he felt. Wherever it was, it wouldn't be the island. He loved the island and the Chandlers and Mate. The thought of leaving them made him feel sick.

Perhaps if he begged them to let him stay, perhaps if he promised—

It wouldn't work. He'd begged and promised the Smiths, but they'd loaded his things into Miss Carr's car and waved good-bye, and he'd never seen them again.

Maybe Aunt Emma would cry, the way Mrs. Smith had. If she did, he'd cry, too. He knew he would, and he was too big a boy now to cry. When the time came to say good-bye to Mate, he just didn't know what he'd do. Mate wouldn't understand. He'd think it was a game. He'd prick up his ears and wag his tail, all eager for the fun to begin. Larry just wouldn't be able to stand that.

It would be better if Miss Carr could come and get him in the middle of the night, when everybody was asleep. Then he wouldn't have to say good-bye to anybody. It would be dark. He wouldn't have to watch the island grow smaller and smaller, as the ferry drew away from it. He wouldn't see the lobster buoys bobbing in the wake of the ferry, and the familiar boats homing into harbor. That would be the best way—best for everybody.

But that wouldn't work, either. The ferry never ran at night. Miss Carr could never be persuaded to ask one of the lobstermen to take them across secretly. She didn't do things that way.

If he could only get across to the main by himself, in the night, and meet Miss Carr at the Stillport landing—

He stopped short in the middle of the sidewalk, so that a fat lady ran into him and said something cranky. Larry didn't hear her. He was absorbed in the beginning of a plan.

Through the days that followed, Larry turned his idea over in his mind. The more he thought about it, the better it seemed. It was only seven miles to the mainland. He could row seven miles. He knew he could. He had rowed Mate clear around the island one fine day, and that was over six miles. He'd take Uncle Joe's skiff, and the ferrymen could bring it back the next day.

Of course, he'd have to leave a note, so that Uncle Joe wouldn't worry about his skiff. He could explain his actions in the note. He didn't want Uncle Joe and

Aunt Emma to think that he'd run away because he didn't like them. He hoped they'd understand how it was.

The only real problem would be the weather. He couldn't pick and choose his time. He had to leave on the night before Miss Carr's next visit. That would be on the Friday after school closed, he knew. He'd have to leave Thursday night. He had to be waiting on the Stillport landing when Miss Carr arrived to take the ferry to the island. She'd make the trip anyhow. She'd have to, to get the other children. She could pick up his clothes and things at the same time. He'd wait in her car while she was gone. He'd rather wait forever than go through those terrible good-byes. Everything would work out fine, if only the weather would co-operate.

Larry was so wrapped up in his plan that the last two weeks of school seemed almost like a dream. He sat at his desk and gave the right answers when Miss Mills called on him, but his thoughts were elsewhere.

On the Saturday before school closed he went out hauling with Uncle Joe. All morning long he thought, This is the last time, ever. The *Petrel* seemed unusually obedient to his hand on the wheel. It was almost as though she knew and was trying to please him.

It was the same with everything else on the island. Familiar things suddenly looked new. He'd forgotten how pretty the harbor was at sunset, with all the boats lying keel to keel with their reflections, until now that

he was seeing it for almost the last time. The kitchen, which he had taken for granted all winter long, was suddenly the most fascinating room in the world. Even the pebbles in the road seemed unusual and beautiful, because they were island pebbles.

Thursday night came at last. The weather was clear and calm. Larry went to his room even earlier than usual. He still had his note to write. He'd been thinking and thinking about it, and he still didn't know what to say. He sat by the window in the last of the daylight, with a pencil and paper, and thought some more.

Finally he began carefully, "Dear Uncle Joe and

Aunt Emma, I know I have to go now school is closed and I don't blame you. I am taking the skiff but don't worry about it Uncle Joe. I will leave it in Stillport with the ferrymen. The reason I am doing it this way is—"

He couldn't find the words to explain that he simply couldn't bear to say good-bye to everybody. It would be easier to say than to write. He'd tell Miss Carr, and she would be able to make them understand. She had always been nice to him, and he trusted her as much as he could trust anyone.

He crossed out the last few words and wrote instead, "Miss Carr will explain things, I will meet her in Stillport tomorrow." That seemed to cover everything, so he signed his name and folded the paper into a neat square.

Then he sat there, watching the dusk creep over the sea. Lights came on in the houses down the road. After a while they went out, one by one. The sky was full of stars, and a crescent moon cast a little light. The sea rumbled gently on the island beaches and ledges. Far off to the west lay the low cloudlike bar that was the mainland.

Ten months ago, Larry remembered, he had looked out this same window at the main and wished that he were there. Well, tomorrow he would be there. He'd give anything in the world now for that not to be true, but it was true. Nothing could change that.

He unfolded the note and placed it on the windowsill. Printing large, because he found it hard to see in the moonlight, he added, "I love you both and Mate." Then he folded it up again, put it in his pocket, and lay down beside Mate to wait, wide-eyed, until it was safe to go.

❦❦ CHAPTER 15

As Larry made his way down to the harbor the night was much darker than he had thought it would be. The moon had set and the stars were dimmed by wisps of cloud. He had escaped the house with no trouble at all. Mate hadn't even waked up when Larry eased himself off the bed and tiptoed down the stairs. He had managed to cross the kitchen without running into anything, and to leave his note under the sugar bowl without clinking any dishes. The kitchen door hadn't creaked, either.

Now if he could get the skiff into the water without too much noise, he'd be all set. Luckily the tide was high, so that the little boat was easy to launch. He climbed in carefully and started paddling with one oar toward the harbor entrance. Sounds carried loudly over water, and the rattle of oars in oarlocks was unmistakable. It would bring any lobsterman who happened to be awake straight down to the shore. There would be time enough for real rowing when he was clear of the island.

Once he had put the channel behind him, Larry took his bearings. He couldn't see much, but the mutter of the lazy surf told him where the ledges were. The mainland lay to the west. He found the polestar by sighting along the edge of the Big Dipper, the way Uncle Joe had taught him. That was north. By keeping the star to the starboard side of the boat, he was bound to head straight west. He picked up the oars and bent his back to rowing.

It was easy at first. The long, slow swells lifted the skiff gently, and the polestar shone bright and constant in the northern sky. The little boat seemed to race across the water. Larry couldn't see the mainland, but he was sure that he must be almost halfway there. It seemed a long time since he had left the harbor.

He paused for a moment to catch his breath and to check his direction. To his dismay, the stars had disappeared. The wisps of cloud had been forerunners of a mass of thick fog. Larry could feel it brushing his face now, and the sleeves of his jacket were beaded with moisture. Alarm swept over him. Without the star to steer by, how could he be sure of his course?

Then he told himself not to be silly. He had been going in the right direction. All he had to do was keep on rowing straight ahead. Sooner or later he was bound to land somewhere on the mainland. When daylight came he could easily find his way to Stillport.

The ferry didn't sail until afternoon. He'd have plenty of time to meet Miss Carr.

He rowed and rowed and rowed. Once he heard the clanging of a bell buoy. He didn't remember any buoy near Stillport, but probably he just hadn't noticed, he decided. The next time he heard it, the sound came from a different direction. Fog, he reminded himself, did funny things to sounds. He had learned that early on the island.

Light began to filter through the darkness. It must be almost morning. Larry could see both ends of the skiff now, but the rest of the world remained shrouded. He seemed to be floating on a little circle of water under a pearly-gray dome. No matter how hard he pulled on the oars, nothing changed. There was still nothing to see except the boat, the water, and the surrounding wall of fog. Surely he ought to have reached the mainland by now.

The motion of the boat changed to a shallow pitching. Larry heard the rumble of surf off to the side. He shipped one of the oars and started paddling with the other. Soon he could touch bottom. He felt a wave of relief. It would be simple to beach the boat in this gentle sea. Then he could walk along the shore until he found someone to direct him. The whole coast around Stillport was thickly settled. There were probably people within shouting distance of him right this minute.

The skiff ran aground as smoothly as Larry had ex-

pected. He jumped out and carried the anchor well ashore, so that the boat would not drift away on the tide. Then he started walking.

The sun was up now. The fog had taken on a golden hue, and he could feel warmth filtering through the dampness. He shouted, hoping someone would hear him, but the only answer was the startled squawking of some sea gulls. He kept on walking. He hoped he would find a house soon. He was beginning to be hungry and thirsty, and time was passing. He had to be in Stillport before Miss Carr got there.

At last he saw a boat drawn up on the shore. That meant that there must be a house nearby. The fog was much thinner now, but he couldn't see any buildings. Probably they were up on the ledges, behind the little stand of fir trees. There'd be a path leading to them from the boat. Larry began to run.

Then he stopped short, unable to believe his eyes. The boat was there all right. The only trouble was that it was Uncle Joe's skiff, right where he himself had left it. He wasn't on the mainland at all. He was on an island, and a small island at that. It had taken him only a short time to go clear around it and back to where he had started.

People who live on islands have boats. He had seen no boat except his own along the whole shore. No one except the gulls had answered his shouts. The truth hit him hard. There was no one here to help him. He was never going to get to Stillport on time. Perhaps he was never going to get there at all.

Larry flung himself on the ground and buried his head in his arms. He lay there for a long time. When he finally sat up, the last of the fog had been burned away by the sun. The wind had come up and was blowing hard. Great breakers crashed against the tiny island. Uncle Joe's skiff was afloat and tugging at the mooring line. In a few more minutes it would have drifted free.

And that would have fixed things good, Larry thought as he tugged it high and dry above the tide line. Without the boat he'd have no way of getting off the island. That is, he thought, unless they came to look for him, as they had for Lon Cole. His heart lifted as he remembered the lobster boats cruising patiently back and forth, and the Coast Guard cutter standing by, and the plane flying over. On Star Island, Uncle Joe had said, they looked out for their own.

But he wasn't one of their own. No matter how much he wished to be, he wasn't an islander. He was only a State Kid that they wanted to get rid of anyhow. If he was going to get off this island, he'd have to do it by himself.

First, he had to find out where he was. From the beach he could see only empty ocean and the surf breaking over a few reefs. He started climbing the ledge behind him. From the top, he'd be able to locate the mainland. When the sea was calmer, he'd start rowing toward it. This time, he'd travel by daylight. Then he could be sure of his direction, and maybe some lobster boat would see him and pick him up. They would probably be willing to put him ashore at Stillport.

What was going to happen after that, he didn't know. He didn't want to think about it. Everybody would be mad at him, of that he was sure. Maybe even Miss Carr would wash her hands of him. He had heard of State Kids who had been put into reformatories for doing things like stealing and running away from foster homes. He supposed, after all, that taking Uncle Joe's boat could be called stealing, even if he hadn't meant it that way.

From the top, Larry could see the whole of his island. As he had guessed, it was very small—little more than a large ledge supporting a few twisted firs, a sparse growth of matted grass, and a great many gulls. They flew over him in a cloud, screaming angrily. He turned so that his back was to the sun and he was facing west. Off toward the horizon he could see several more islands. Strain his eyes as he might, though, there was no sign of the long, dark line of the mainland.

He turned and looked the other way, but there was nothing except empty ocean. He must have got turned around in the fog and spent most of the night rowing straight out to sea, he realized. That meant that one of the islands to the west was Star, but he had no idea which one. They were too far away to be anything but hazy shapes against the blue.

There was only one thing to do—wait until the wind went down and the sea was calmer, and row to one of those islands. Any one of them would be better than this. At least it would be large enough to have fresh water on it somewhere. He was getting terribly thirsty, and there was nothing at all to drink here. He might have a long wait, though. The wind usually came up with the sun, blew all day, and went down when the sun went down. He might have to wait until earliest light the next day before setting out. He didn't know whether he could last that long without a drink of water.

He'd better find a place to sit down out of the sun. Its rays were hot, in spite of the breeze. He pulled a long stalk of grass and chewed on it as he settled down in the scanty shade of the fir trees. Chewing the grass helped his thirst some, but not much.

Off in the distance he could see some white specks that he knew were lobster boats. One of them might even be Uncle Joe. It seemed a year since he had seen Uncle Joe and Aunt Emma and Mate. Yet it was only last night. He wondered if they missed him as much as he was missing them, and if they were worried about him. Not worried enough to start looking for him, he decided. Those boats out there weren't searching for anything. He could tell by their movements that they were simply going about their regular business, cruising from trap to trap.

Anyhow, it wasn't time yet for anyone to worry. Uncle Joe and Aunt Emma had read his note long before now, and they must think that he was safe in Stillport. They wouldn't know that he was missing until the ferry reached Star Island and they talked with Miss Carr, some time this afternoon.

The thought of Miss Carr encouraged him. He wasn't an islander, so maybe the islanders wouldn't be interested in what became of him. But he was a State Kid, and Miss Carr was a state caseworker. She was responsible for him. She had to see that he was found. If she went back to the office and said that she was sorry, but she had lost one of her charges, they'd probably fire her. Miss Carr wouldn't like that at all. If for no other reason, she'd make sure that he was found.

Somewhat comforted by this thought, Larry fell asleep. He had been up all night, he had rowed a long way, and he was tired. The thick mattress of fir needles on which he lay was soft, and the sound of the surf was soothing. In spite of his thirst and his worries, his eyes closed.

He dreamed that he heard the familiar throb of the *Petrel*'s engine coming closer and closer, and then Uncle Joe's voice calling his name. It was so real that he sat up with a jerk and answered the call before he realized where he was or remembered all that had happened. It was funny, he thought, how lifelike some

144

dreams could be. He could still hear the sound of the motor, lingering on from his sleep.

Uncle Joe's voice came again, strong and clear. It wasn't a dream. It was true! The sun was straight overhead, so it was only noon. The ferry hadn't even started for Star Island with Miss Carr aboard. Yet Uncle Joe was here, looking for him. He couldn't possibly be, but he was.

Larry raced down to the shore, shouting every step of the way. He was half afraid that he was still dreaming or that his ears were playing tricks on him. But there was the *Petrel,* circling in close, with Uncle Joe standing on the engine housing for a better view, and old Perley Stevens at the wheel—old Perley, with his head full of things that could come in handy on a search.

❧❧ CHAPTER 16

As he rowed from the beach to the *Petrel*, Larry tried to think what he was going to say to Uncle Joe. He would say he was sorry, of course. He had made Uncle Joe waste a whole morning of good hauling weather. But after that, what? Everything was the same as it had been yesterday. There were still the good-byes that he had tried to avoid. The only difference was that he had made a lot of trouble for everyone. Nobody was going to like him any better for that, or be sorrier to see the last of him.

Uncle Joe saved him the embarrassment of having to speak first. "Welcome aboard," he said drily. "I ain't going to bawl you out, so you can quit looking like a whipped pup. I'll save that for Ma. She's going to climb up one side of you and down the other, I'm warning you. I don't envy you the next few hours after we go ashore, I can tell you that. When she ain't letting you feel the sharp edge of her tongue, she'll be

146

crying and weeping over you and trying to put you to bed with a hot-water bottle. I don't know which is worse. I ain't trying to scare you. I'm just preparing you for what's to come."

Larry stared at Uncle Joe in surprise. It wasn't like him to run on and on like this. Then he realized with amazement that Uncle Joe was talking to cover up his own feelings. He had been worried. He was so glad to see Larry that he almost didn't know what he was saying.

Uncle Joe was still talking. "The time Carl ran away, Ma carried on so over him that I hid down in the shop till well past dark. I didn't have any supper and didn't go home till I was sure the storm had blown over. I tell you, women—"

Larry interrupted. "*Carl* ran away?" Larry couldn't understand it. Carl belonged on the island.

"Yup, and me in my day, and I'll bet old Perley here—"

Larry had almost forgotten the old man until he spoke up. "I made it to the main, and my pa was waiting for me there. Seventy-six years ago, that was, and I ain't forgot to this day the way my ma took on." Perley shook his head.

"But *why* did you run away?" Larry asked.

"You'd ought to know," Uncle Joe told him, "considering that you just done the same thing yourself. All island boys are the same. They begin to feel boxed in. They want to see the rest of the world. So some fine day they take off, like you did. Some of us get over the notion, like Perley and me did. Some, like Carl, don't. Either way, it's something all island boys go through, one time or another."

"But it wasn't that way with me," Larry said. "I didn't run away because I didn't like the island. It was because I liked it too much."

Uncle Joe looked at him. "I guess you're going to have to explain that. Sounds like sort of a funny reason to me." He wasn't cross. He really wanted to know.

"Well, you were going to send me back with Miss Carr today anyhow, and I couldn't stand—"

Uncle Joe looked completely dumbfounded. "What in tunket ever gave you a crazy idea like that?"

"School's over," Larry said. It seemed to him that ought to explain everything, but Uncle Joe seemed more puzzled than ever.

Larry tried again. "You don't need us State Kids anymore. Mr. Vance said at Christmas that the only reason you took us was to keep the school. Now school's over. Why should you bother with us?"

Uncle Joe was speechless, but old Perley said softly and wonderingly, "The loony notions young ones get in their heads!"

"It's not loony," Larry disputed hotly. Suddenly he didn't feel like a young one, but like a man talking to equals. "You've never been a State Kid, neither one of you. I've been one all my life. I know what I'm talking about, better'n you'll ever know. People use

148

you, then they get rid of you. As far back as I can remember—"

He went on in a rush, telling them about the Smiths
and the Whites and the Frosts and all the others. He
told them things he had never thought he would say
out loud; how he had hoped so hard at first, and
then had learned to hope less, and finally not to hope
at all. At last he stopped and stood staring blindly
through the spray shield at the dazzling sea.

There was a long moment of silence, broken only
by the purr of the *Petrel*'s engine and the wash of the
waves. Then old Perley cleared his throat. "So that's
how folks are on the main," he said in his thin, old-
man's voice.

"Not the bulk of them. Larry's just had bad luck."

That was like Uncle Joe, Larry thought. He always tried to be fair.

"Larry, let's get a few things straight." Uncle Joe was very serious. "About this school business. What Horry Vance said was true. But it was only part of the truth. If he'd had time— You remember the ferry hove in sight when he was halfway through his speech? If he'd had time to finish, he'd have said that you state young ones have been a blessing to us islanders, that you've given us all a new interest in life and made us all feel young and alive again, and that when summer came, we'd show our appreciation. I know that's what he was going to say, because he told me so. More than once—me and anyone else who'd listen. If anything riles Horry, it's being cut off in the middle of one of his speeches."

"Amen!" said Perley with feeling. "But this once he was going to say something worth hearing. Why, even me, living alone like the worthless old coot that I am, even me, I see the change you young ones have made in the island. We wouldn't trade a one of you for all the tea in China. And I like tea as well as anybody."

"That's another thing," Uncle Joe said. "Ma and me, we've grown as fond of you as if you were our own. It never crossed our minds but what you'd be with us permanent. When the time comes, you'll go over to the main for high school, of course. But when you come back, I figured you and me'd lobster together. Partners, like. That is, if you've a mind to. I'll be getting along in years then. I used to think that Carl and me— But it didn't work out that way."

Larry couldn't believe that Uncle Joe meant what he was saying. "You mean live with you and Aunt Emma on the island forever? Oh, Uncle Joe!" He stopped, afraid that he was going to cry. He was too big a boy for that, he remembered in time.

Old Perley saved the situation. "Watch your step, boy," he said solemnly. "By the time we get in harbor, Joe's going to have you married and naming your first young one after him."

They were approaching Star Island now. Larry looked at the familiar outline with new eyes. All the rest of his life he would be coming home to it. Even the winters when Uncle Joe said he'd have to go to high school in Stillport wouldn't be so bad. He could get through the days, knowing that as sure as Friday afternoon rolled around he'd be going back to the island for the weekend. He and Matt and Sally and Tom, because of course they'd all be together. Even if Tom and Sally left the island when they grew up, there'd always be Matt. Matt was like Perley and Uncle Joe. He'd never want to live on the main, Larry was sure.

Why, he and Matt were going to be lifelong friends! From now on they could share everything. He had never expected to have a friendship that would endure for a lifetime. It was too big an idea to accept all at once. Maybe he'd never be able to believe it completely. Maybe that would be best. That way, he'd never forget to be thankful.

Suddenly something occurred to him. "How did you know where to look for me? I didn't see the Coast Guard plane."

"Didn't call the Coast Guard. Soon's Ma and I found your note and I seen what a miserable, foggy morning it was, I knew you'd never get to the main. Nobody— not you nor me nor anybody else—can row a straight line in a fog without a compass. Everybody pulls a little harder on one oar than on the other. On top of that, there are currents out here to take a man off course. So I went down and got Perley."

"You're probably wondering why he picked a worthless old has-been like me," Perley commented with great good nature.

"Uncle Joe told me once that you had an awful lot of things stored in your head that would come in handy on a search."

"Yup, I have," Perley stated smugly, pleased with the compliment. "There ain't no more knowledgeable man on the coast of Maine than me, when it comes to winds and currents."

"The way I figured," Uncle Joe went on, "if we could find you before anyone else knew you were gone, so much the better. That Miss Carr's a good woman, a fine woman, but she works for the state. For all I know, the state may have notions and rules about boys who run away from places where the state says they ought to stay. I didn't know, and I didn't aim to find out."

"So he come to me," Perley continued the story. "I knew as well as I needed to pretty nigh where you'd be. There's a strong current sweeps right out to Gull Island, where you were. Course, you might have missed it—"

"What would you have done then?" If he was going to be a lobsterman, Larry thought, he wanted to know all about everything. He wanted to be as smart as Perley, when he was that old.

"Oh, we'd have gee-hawed around for a couple of hours. Then if we didn't find you, we'd have called the Coast Guard. But as it turned out, we didn't have to."

"Then nobody at all knows about me?"

They were entering the channel now, and Uncle Joe's attention was on the markers. Then he said, "Nope, nobody but Ma. They all think you'n me'n Perley went out hauling together today. We left before anybody else was down to the shore."

He tied the *Petrel* to her mooring and pulled the skiff alongside. "Get in," he said to Perley. "Larry can row us ashore. He's had a lot a practice during the night."

Perley cackled. "One thing," he said as he clambered out onto the bench. "The reason I got so much in my head is that I ain't got a big mouth. What goes in my head stays there. You've got nothing to worry about as far as I'm concerned. Emma, now, she's another matter. You'd do well to start worrying about what she's going to say and do to you." He cackled again and walked away.

Uncle Joe looked after him. "He ain't joking. Ma's liable to give you a hard time, Larry. Of course, what you printed at the end of your note might make some difference. Some, but not much—not first off. I been thinking. If I was to go up to the house with you and sort of take your side, tell her some of the things about your life on the main that you were telling Perley and me—"

Larry felt like hugging him. He just loved Uncle Joe. But he shook his head. "Nope," he said. "I'll go alone. She can't more than half kill me." He didn't add how nice it was to know that someone cared enough about him to half kill him.

Besides, he was an island boy. Running away and being punished for it was something all island boys had to go through, one time or another. This was his time. He might as well get it over with.

He grinned at Uncle Joe and started up the road toward Aunt Emma and home.